ROLANDO CÁRDENAS

On the Life and Work of a Chilean Master

RECENT BOOKS IN THE UNSUNG MASTERS SERIES

2025

Rosemary Catacalos: On the Life and Work of an American Master
Edited by Jim LaVilla-Havelin & Maha Ahmed

2024

Tom Postell: On the Life and Work of an American Master
Edited by Michael C. Peterson & Anthony Sutton

2023

Bert Meyers: On the Life and Work of an American Master
Edited by Dana Levin & Adele Elise Williams

2022

Jean Ross Justice: On the Life and Work of an American Master
Edited by Ryan Bollenbach & Kevin Prufer

2021

Shreela Ray: On the Life and Work of an American Master
Edited by Kazim Ali & Rohan Chhetri

2020

Wendy Battin: On the Life and Work of an American Master
Edited by Charles Hartman, Martha Collins, Pamela Alexander, & Matthew Krajniak

2019

Laura Hershey: On the Life and Work of an American Master
Edited by Meg Day & Niki Herd

2018

Adelaide Crapsey: On the Life and Work of an American Master
Edited by Jenny Molberg & Christian Bancroft

Additional titles available at **www.unsungmasters.org**

GULF COAST
A JOURNAL OF LITERATURE AND FINE ARTS

inprint
INSPIRING READERS & WRITERS

PLEIADES PRESS

UNIVERSITY of HOUSTON

Cu Ni

PLOUGHSHARES AT EMERSON COLLEGE

THE UNSUNG MASTERS SERIES

Series Editors:

Kevin Prufer, Martin Rock, & Wayne Miller

Cárdenas Has Died

by Jorge Teillier

The poet Lorenzo Peirano came from Coinco
to Esperanza Street, through the breathing alleys
he wrote about, & sent me a telegram:

« *Murió Cárdenas* »

We saw each other for the last time
on the 18th of September in Inés de Suárez Park,
the city was waving flags in honor of this encounter.
Now, I can only hope that next we'll meet
together with Samuel Donoso,
to read Saint-John Perse & sing:

« *Oh qué dulce es el misterio de la vida* »

Wait for me, Rolando. You have given the sign.

Translated by Mathew Weitman

Rolando Cárdenas: On the Life & Work of a Chilean Master

ISBN: 978-1-7344356-6-5
Published by The Unsung Masters Series in collaboration with *Gulf Coast*, *Copper Nickel*, *Pleiades,* and *Ploughshares.*

Department of English
University of Houston
Houston, TX 77204

Produced at the University of Houston and Inprint

Distributed by Asterism and to subscribers of *Pleiades: Literature in Context, Ploughshares,* and *Gulf Coast: A Journal of Literature and Fine Arts.*

www.asterismbooks.com/publisher/the-unsung-masters-series

Series, cover, and interior design by Martin Rock.
Cover photograph by Jorge Aravena Llanca. Courtesy of the photographer.

2 4 6 8 9 7 5 3 1
First Printing, 2026

The Unsung Masters Series brings the work of great, out-of-print, little-known writers to new readers. Each volume in the Series includes a large selection of the author's original writing, as well as essays on the writer, interviews with people who knew the writer, photographs, and ephemera. The curators of The Unsung Masters Series are always interested in suggestions for future volumes.

Underwriting support provided by Inprint,
thanks to board member Debbie Gary.
Also by the University of Houston English Department

UNIVERSITY of **HOUSTON**

ROLANDO CÁRDENAS

On the Life and Work
of a Chilean Master

Edited by FELIPE ACEVEDO RIQUELME,
MATHEW WEITMAN, and JULY WESTHALE

CONTENTS

Letters from the Editors

FROM JULY:

IN JULY OF 2005 I sat in an artificially bright, windowless room in the literature department of the Pontificia Universidad Católica in Santiago, Chile. It was winter, and the dry, dirty cold turned our breath into wispy shapes. Few among us—the exchange students from various universities in California—were paying attention to Paula, the dark-haired girl running through a list of tactical information on a clipboard: class matriculation deadlines, where to pay tuition, how to take the Metro. She seemed to understand this. She wrapped up her logistics snappishly, gesturing in the direction of her colleague next to her, a bored-seeming misanthrope with a long scarf wound around his neck. "This is a typical Chilean male."

"Spin," Paula said. He glared at her and then out at us.

This is how I met Felipe Acevedo Riquelme, one of the co-editors of this collection. And in meeting Felipe, I was set on course to encounter the poetry of Rolando Cárdenas. It was not long before he was pointing out the glaring flaws in my Poetic Theory class—no Magellanic poets—and inviting me on a walk through one of Santiago's outdoor book fairs. He sent directions over email, with the post-script "if you get lost, text me, and I will get lost with you."

The combination of getting lost together and loving books, nearly above all else, created a strong baseline for friendship. Over decades and continents, we have been most content reading out loud to one another in ornate Chilean courtyards, walking miles in the rain to English cemeteries to find the resting places of poets, or laying on our backs under the stars in the driest desert in the world, trying to recite poems from memory that could capture the magnitude of the world and our smallness inside of it. Once, when we were still students, I took a bus for ten days to visit him in Punta Arenas, the hometown he shared with Rolando Cárdenas. We drank leche con plátano and ate choripán and he showed me where his friends, many gone now, taught him how to ride a bike. We watched the ships come and go, the same ships, I like to think, that so alluded and fascinated Cárdenas.

Experiencing Cárdenas' haunts was easier than finding his poetry. The primary challenge of being a literature student in Chile in the aughts was one of access. The crushing censorship under the Pinochet regime, coupled with the inaccessibility of education, made finding books not only extraordinarily difficult but also prohibitively expensive, should you be able to find them at all. Considering cost and scarcity, students were not expected to purchase the books listed on their syllabi. Instead, we were told to go to one of several kiosks located inside the university where, upon sharing the course numbers of the classes we were taking, we were given a folio of photocopied materials, paying only for the cost of printing and binding.

Somehow, I was able to find one poem by Rolando Cárdenas—"Tierra del Fuego"—on the internet, using the library computer, or my ancient Dell, connecting to the subway's free wifi. Still, I couldn't find a complete book of Cárdenas poems anywhere.

In December of 2006, Pinochet died. He'd been under indictment for crimes against humanity but never sentenced. I was living in Santiago Centro, down the street from La Alameda, where protestors and mourners alike gathered to watch his funerary cavalcade march through the city's beating heart. There were celebrations and half-mast flags on flagrant display, often in the same neighborhood. The next year, I moved back to California.

The dictatorship effectively ended in 1990—seven months and six days before Cárdenas died—but it wasn't until Pinochet's death that the country began to change the way it discussed its own histories. The atrocities committed by the regime became a part of the country's story, writ large and memorialized through institutions like the *Museum of Memory and Human Rights* (est. 2010). Here, visitors can find information about the era surrounding the Pinochet regime and search for disappeared family members. Names of the disappeared are also memorialized at Patio 29, a mass grave of political victims and prisoners established at Santiago's General Cemetery.

In 2017, on his first visit to see me in Oakland, Felipe brought a paper-wrapped gift with him—*Obra Completa*, by Rolando Cárdenas, compiled by Ramón Díaz Eterovic, a fellow writer from Punta Areas who admired his work. *Obra Completa* was published posthumously, in 1994. It contains five collections: *Brief Transits, In the Winter of the Province,*

Characters of My City, Migratory Poems, Vast Empires and *What, Behind Those Walls*. Felipe had discovered it in a rare book store in Santiago. This feels notable: despite everything that began to feel possible after Pinochet's death, the books of writers censored by the dictatorship were extraordinarily difficult to find.

The poems contained in *Obra Completa* demonstrate breathtaking renditions of Chilean landscapes: bucolic, metropolitan, and political alike. With most of Cárdenas' work situated promptly before the 1973 coup d'état—and implicitly reckoning with its aftermath—the volumes are enmeshed in the inter-workings of a country divided by class struggle, existential and cultural crisis, and regionalism. And as with the most impactful poetic works, the true artistry of Rolando Cárdenas is his ability to bring the sharpness and duality of a country under siege to light with stunning alacrity. Cárdenas did not explicitly write about the dictatorship, or its deleterious impacts on his own life. However, his literary career never gained the due nor visibility it was on track to earning. He suffered greatly, personally and professionally. And while we can only speculate, it feels notable that the dictatorship ended the same year he died.

* * *

THAT CÁRDENAS HAS NOT BEEN TRANSLATED for a wider audience is a gross oversight, most certainly owing to the tumultuous political history in which he found himself; his poetry is a vital part of Chile's story and literary canon. By bringing his work to an international audience, we hope to offer a more robust understanding of Chilean political history: Cárdenas's story complicates the one often told.

Unlike other poets of the era, he was not killed during the coup, or exiled after; instead, this is the story of a poet who stayed, at great cost to himself. Even our editorial team—me, Felipe, Mathew—had difficulty procuring copies of *Obra Completa* to start the translation process. Mathew, based in Texas, received his copy much more quickly than Felipe did, who is based in Concepción, Chile.

* * *

THE STORY OF THE COUP and the ensuing Pinochet dictatorship, the story of how it became a hero's journey to find books written by some of the greatest unsung Chilean masters—these stories are in keeping with the stories Jorge Aravena Llanca tells of his own friendship with the poet. For Cárdenas, community was every bit as poignant as his precious solitude, and the space between public and private often live comfortably next to one another in his work; in his poem "La Búsqueda" (*The Search*), he wrote: "It is good to sit amongst friends and glasses / and observe how everyone abandons something of themselves." The speaker is both alone and connected to the alone-ness of everyone in the room. A few stanzas down, the speaker is gently reminded of time passing and how it is marked by observing others: "It is good to understand that we are made of memory, / that time grows without listening to us. / That there are many things we do not understand." His connection to friendship as the true nexus of all art is in keeping with the stories he told those in his life—Jorge, Ramón Díaz Eterovic—about his relationship with his writing.

The story of friendship and scarcity and true, abiding love of art, the commitment to poetry and the poet behind the poems—it didn't start with this project. While it is true that the journey to put this manuscript together was one that reflected the realities and generosity of art and love that marked Rolando Cárdenas' life and work, it is also true that this work preceded us by at least decades. Before the seed of this book even began (in 2017, when Felipe handed me my deeply treasured copy, or maybe even in 2005 when we met at university), there were those who loved and venerated this vital poet. We owe a great debt to them. Ramon Diaz Eterovic's *Obra Completa* was the first book of Cárdenas' work post-dictatorship, pulling together his entire life's work, including poems that had never before been published. We also benefitted greatly from the photos, reflections, and homages to the poet by Jorge Aravena Llanca, Jorge Teillier, and others. This also led to the comparatively vast Cárdenas archive in the National Library, which is full of poem drafts, photos, letters, and other biographical materials that were not available in 2005 when I first encountered the poet's work.

On the subject of how Cárdenas' constellation of community helped to shape this Unsung Masters book, a note on the editorial process: when considering whether or not to include a traditional bibliography of source material, Mathew, Felipe, and I reckoned with the stunning fact that, while this collection references some traditional resources (newspapers, essays, etc.), it is also built foundationally on the backs of story and memory. Ramón Díaz Eterovic himself was enthusiastic, quick, and willing to communicate with me at every turn, sharing with us the contact information for photographers and other Cárdenas' loved ones. He did everything in his power to help bring this poet's work the much-deserved (and long overdue) acclaim it deserved. Jorge Aravena Llanca not only provided us with the lion's share of the photographs and letters included here, he also allowed us the use of the song and agreed to let Felipe interview him; this extraordinary conversation is the beating heart of this collection, and without it we would not be able to place the full impact of Cárdenas' life and work. "María Cecilia Ojeda Cárdenas, Rolando's niece knew how precious and vital his legacy was; she made this all possible by granting us permission to translate from his estate. Additionally, we would like to thank the Departamento de Idiomas Extranjeros of the Universidad de Concepción, especially its Chair, Boris Pradel Suárez, as well as the coordinadores de práctica profesional, Cristina González Riquelme and Cristian Martínez Carvajal, for their ongoing support of this project. Our deepest gratitude goes to Daniela Jara and Valentina Merino, whose dedicated work as part of their professional translator training was fundamental to the completion of this book. Family, friends, and fellow writers created this archive of memory, mastery, and feeling you hold. Thank you for being here with us.

FROM MATHEW:

ONE YEAR AGO, while attempting to bring some of Jorge Teillier's most intertextual poems into English for the first time, I was struck by a rather mysterious poem in memoriam of a rather obscure poet. Though much of the work I was translating was full of allusions and dedications to the French Symbolists, lyric poets such as George Trakl and Henry Treece, and many of the most prominent Spanish language poets of the 20th century—Antonio Machado, Pablo Neruda, Rosamel de Valle—something about this poem, titled "Murió Cárdenas," seemed deeply personal, unknowable, and (at the time) untranslatable. That I should first encounter Rolando Cárdenas through one of his many lasting friendships feels—for lack of a better word—perfect.

The quest to obtain the materials and permissions for this volume has not only led me to many wonderful places but also introduced me to many wonderful people that I wish to acknowledge beyond the confines of MLA citational practice. While creating the biographical timeline for this anthology, I relied heavily on the resources digitally available in the Biblioteca Nacional de Chile. This digital archival work directly led to my "discovery" of three hard to find translations by Miller Williams (until now, the only Cárdenas poetry available in English). As luck would have it—and this was often the case with this project—I was able to view these materials at the Harry Ransom Center and Benson Latin American Collection at the University of Texas, Austin (just a few hours from my desk in Houston). I am grateful to Rebecca Jordan Williams for granting us permission to include her late husband's work—and to Meghan Hoefling and Cathy Henderson for getting us in touch. I would also like to thank Sebastian Teillier for granting us permission to translate his father's poem, which functions as an epigraph to this volume.

Though Rolando Cárdenas never directly wrote about his experiences as an incarcerated citizen, as July, Felipe, and I worked our way through these archival materials, conversations, and ephemera, it became increasingly evident that there are profound reverberations in his silence. Like many victims of the 1973 coup d'état, the story of Cárdenas's life was quite nearly erased with his work. As such, I wish to thank the curators and researchers at Santiago's Museum of Memory and Human Rights, who have archived the atrocities that took place under Augusto Pinochet's decades-long regime. This organization is devoted to recovering the lost stories and voices of hundreds of thousands of Chilean citizens; in so doing, they have created an educational space that directly challenges our understanding of "history" as a stable construct.

With this same spirit, The Unsung Masters Series has continually destabilized "the canon" by bringing the work of overlooked, understudied, and out-of-print authors back into the literary discourse. This commitment to archival research has not only exposed the tacit prejudices embedded within such "canon building," but has also formed an intricate network of researchers, scholars, and writers across sixteen incredible volumes (and many more to come). On behalf of my coeditors, Rolando Cárdenas, and all who were lucky enough to know him, I want to extend my deepest thanks to The Unsung Masters Series Editors: Kevin Prufer, Wayne Miller, and Martin Rock. We would also like to thank Debbie Gary, whose financial support made this project possible, and the language department of the University of Concepción; many of the long-form prose translations were the work of student translators, credited by name throughout the collection.

Each of these inspiring human beings and resources remain invaluable to my work as a translator and researcher of Chilean poetry, in addition to my work as an educator in carceral settings. To this end, I wish to extend my unending gratitude to Rich Levy, Krupa Parikh, and Tayyba Kanwal at Inprint, who have worked tirelessly with me for the past four years to sustain ongoing creative writing programming in carceral settings throughout the greater Houston area. I'm also deeply thankful to Will Lowder, who helped me edit and assemble numerous anthologies of poetry written by my students at the Harris County Jail. These experiences directly informed every decision I made as a coeditor, researcher, and translator of this volume. It is a privilege to be a part of this project, and to share the work of this silent—but never silenced—poet.

FROM FELIPE:

Translating Rolando Cárdenas: Survival, Community, and Repair

I first came to the poetry of Rolando Cárdenas in adolescence, thanks to my high school literature teacher, Moira Aicón. She believed that if we were to read Jorge Teillier as part of the program she had designed for us, we also had to know Cárdenas, because as Magellanic readers his voice belonged to us in a different, more intimate way. She also considered him a poet who deserved to be remembered. The year was 2001. This coincided with the reissue of his *Obra Completa*, edited by writer (and now Chilean National Literature Prize laureate) Ramón Díaz Eterovic, another native of Punta Arenas who deeply admired Cárdenas. That moment marked my first approach to a poet who, though from my own land, reached me as an elusive, almost secret figure.

Today, more than twenty years later, I find myself working as co-editor of the English translation of that same work for The Unsung Masters Series, dedicated to authors who have not been celebrated or disseminated in a "just" manner. I think of this trajectory as a kind of circular journey: from my first encounter in a high school classroom to the current effort to bring his poetry into global circuits. And I ask myself whether it is not translation, precisely, that might offer Cárdenas the possibility of a new life and of historical repair.

I believe in translation as a strategy of survival and justice. Following Walter Benjamin, every translation prolongs the "afterlife" of a text, though always provisionally and in transformation. Here, Cárdenas is paradigmatic: forgotten or relegated in his own language, translation could open the door to a second life, perhaps more visible than the first. Translating him thus becomes a gesture of poetic justice in the face of silence and marginalization.

As scholars such as Lawrence Venuti, Emily Apter, or André Lefevere have noted, translation is never neutral. It is a political and comparative act, since it mediates between languages and cultures, but it also intervenes in the dynamics of visibility and legitimacy that determine which voices resonate and which remain marginalized. Translating Rolando Cárdenas disputes those literary maps and reclaims a poetic archive that, without such mediation, would remain confined to limited editorial circulation and local memory.

Hence, translation may be understood as an act of cultural repair: a way of safeguarding the dignity of silenced voices and granting them a second life in another language, while keeping in view their silences, their absences, and the traces of a convulsive historical time.

* * *

Rolando Cárdenas and Invisibility

TO SPEAK OF ROLANDO CÁRDENAS is also to speak of an experience of reading marked by distance and difficulty. Although he published six books between 1956 and 1988, his work never consolidated in national circulation. His figure remained confined to regional memory and to the friendship of writers such as Jorge Teillier, Jorge Aravena Llanca, and other regulars of La Unión Chica bar, without achieving the institutional legitimacy that other poets of his generation did attain.

After his death in 1990, the first posthumous edition of his *Obras Completa* appeared in 1994, published by La Gota Pura and compiled by Ramón Díaz Eterovic. Years later, in 2001, the Corporación Cultural del Sur released a second edition. This was also edited by Díaz Eterovic, which allowed his poems to circulate once again, although in moderate print runs and with limited distribution. More than two decades later, it is still practically impossible to find these volumes outside used bookstores or specialized archives.

This difficulty of access, which has already been underscored in the testimonial notes of July Westhale and Mathew Weitman as part of their own editorial and archival experience, also constitutes a critical dimension of Cárdenas's marginal condition in Chilean literature. Here I aim to take up these observations within a sort of theoretical framework: limited access is not only a material obstacle but also a symptom of cultural and political invisibility.

Historical conditions exacerbated this invisibility. Pinochet's dictatorship (1973 – 1990) violently disrupted democratic life and literary circulation alike: censorship, exile, economic crisis, and cultural repression severely restricted access to books. Within that context, Cárdenas's work was relegated even further, until it became almost spectral—surviving in inaccessible libraries, in scattered photocopies, or in the memory of his friends.

His death in 1990—just months after the formal end of the dictatorship—symbolizes, in a way, this truncated destiny. As July points out eloquently, Cárdenas did not live to see the slow opening of spaces of memory and repair that would emerge in democracy. His voice remained caught in an interstice: too soon to be recovered, too late to consolidate during his lifetime.

From the present moment, this oblivion has a double edge. On the one hand, it deprives readers of a poet who articulated like few others the solitude and disquiet of the southernmost region. On the other hand, by being excluded from the canon, his work risks disappearing altogether from cultural memory. Here is where translation emerges not as a belated supplement, but as a strategy of survival. In other words: a way to grant Cárdenas a second life, both in English and in Spanish, returning resonance to a voice that was silenced.

* * *

Translation as Survival and Justice

AS I HAVE MENTIONED, thinking about the translation of Rolando Cárdenas means, above all, asking how a poet who has been practically forgotten in his own language might find in another a space of survival. Translation, in this sense, is not a mere transfer of words but an act that prolongs, reconfigures, and repairs.

Benjamin[1], in "The Task of the Translator," anticipated this by noting that translations prolong the "afterlife" of texts. I mentioned this previously. What this means: a work does not die when it ceases to circulate in its original language; on the contrary, it may find in translation a new vitality, an afterlife. If we consider Cárdenas—whose poems remain inaccessible in Chile and whose books are almost impossible to obtain—translating him into English becomes a way of guaranteeing

[1] Benjamin, Walter. "The Task of the Translator." Translated by Harry Zohn. *Selected Writings: Volume 1, 1913 – 1926*, edited by Marcus Bullock and Michael W. Jennings, Harvard UP, 1996, pp. 253 – 63. Originally published 1923.

the continuity that maybe the Spanish of his own country has somewhat denied him.

This prolongation, however, must not be understood as fixation. Jacques Derrida[2] reminds us that every translation is iterative and unfinished: no version can exhaust the meaning of the original, because each attempt opens new possibilities of reading. Translating Cárdenas is not about crystallizing his voice but about accepting that his work can and must continue multiplying in other languages, resisting silence through its own re-opening. Survival, in this framework, is not immobility but movement.

If translation guarantees that afterlife, it also defines the conditions of visibility. Jenny Williams[3] recalls that the history of translation theory in the West has oscillated between two poles: the literalism defended by the so-called *sourcerers* and the interpretive freedom of the *targeteers*. This debate, far from being purely technical, reveals relations of power between languages and cultures. As Alexander Pope noted in his preface to *The Iliad*, literalism never does justice to an "excellent" original in a supposedly superior language, reproducing cultural hierarchies. Translating Cárdenas confronts us directly with this dilemma: how to avoid domesticating his Magellanic language to the point of erasure, while ensuring that his images breathe in another tongue?

---

[2] Derrida, Jacques. "What Is a 'Relevant' Translation?" Translated by Lawrence Venuti. *The Translation Studies Reader*, edited by Lawrence Venuti, 4th ed., Routledge, 2021, pp. 365 – 88. Originally published 1985.

[3] Williams, Jenny. "Theory and Literary Translation Practice." *The Routledge Handbook of Literary Translation*, edited by Lawrence Raw, Routledge, 2018, pp. 78 – 92.

The non-Western perspective offers a decisive counterpoint. As Sujit Mukherjee and A.K. Ramanujan points out—as cited by Williams—in India translation has often been conceived not in terms of literalism or freedom but as *transcreation*: a practice that infuses new life into texts and recognizes the translator as creator. Applied to Cárdenas, this idea allows us to think of translation as a kind of reincarnation. Each version is a new incarnation of his voice, different but still linked to its origin. From this angle, translation does not compete with the original but multiplies it.

This gesture, however, is not exempt from ethical tensions. Gayatri Spivak[4] warns us that translating subaltern or peripheral voices always carries the risk of erasure. A translation that is too fluent or domesticated may strip away what makes a text unique. Hence the need for careful attention to linguistic texture and opacity. Retaining certain words in Spanish or resisting the temptation to smooth the rhythms of southern Spanish is not a minor philological detail but a form of justice against oblivion, ensuring that difference survives.

Similarly, Emily Apter[5] warns against the temptation of a homogenized "world literature" in which everything is translated toward a single center. Her proposal is to think of translation as resistance: not as passive integration into the

[4] Spivak, Gayatri Chakravorty. "The Politics of Translation." *The Translation Studies Reader,* edited by Lawrence Venuti, 4th ed., Routledge, 2021, pp. 387 – 416. Originally published 1992. [5] Apter, Emily. *Against World Literature: On the Politics of Untranslatability.* Verso, 2013.

[5] Apter, Emily. *Against World Literature: On the Politics of Untranslatability.* Verso, 2013.

global market but as a way of preserving difference. Cárdenas is revealing here: forgotten in Spanish, he finds in translation a new life. But that new life must not mean absorption into a global canon without nuance; rather, it must inscribe him as a southern, peripheral voice marked by exposure.

Addressing this same conundrum, Kwame Appiah[6] deepens this ethical dimension by proposing *thick translation.* A "dense" translation does not merely transfer meanings; it contextualizes, explains, and thickens cultural experience. For a poet like Cárdenas, anchored in the geography and history of Magallanes, translation demands precisely that: notes, references, mediations that allow Anglophone readers to access a distinct culture without erasing its density, similar to what we attempt to do in this book with the interviews, comments and ephemera we have included.

In parallel, Lefevere[7] reminds us that every translation is also a rewriting. It is not an isolated act, but a practice conditioned by patronage, ideologies, and literary systems. The translation of Cárdenas must be understood in that network: the will of his heirs, the mediation of editors and critics, the persistence of archives and memories. Each of these instances shapes the way his voice survives.

Together, these perspectives invite us to conceive translation not as a technical operation but as an act of

---

[6] Appiah, Kwame Anthony. "Thick Translation." *The Translation Studies Reader*, edited by Lawrence Venuti, 4th ed., Routledge, 2021, pp. 331 – 43. Originally published 2000.

[7] Lefevere, André. "Mother Courage's Cucumbers: Text, System, and Refraction in a Theory of Literature." *The Translation Studies Reader*, edited by Lawrence Venuti, 4th ed., Routledge, 2021, pp. 233 – 49. Originally published 1982.

revitalization and cultural justice. Once again, translating Cárdenas means prolonging his voice beyond oblivion, multiplying it in new languages without erasing its roughness, and attempting to make space for it on a literary map where it can coexist, finally, with other poets without remaining at the margins. Translation, in this case, is repair, the gesture that ensures that a poet seemingly condemned to silence has the chance to keep breathing.

* * *

The Cárdenas Translation Project: Community, Affection, and Repair

FROM THE BEGINNING, the translation of Rolando Cárdenas's complete works was marked by a singular decision: not to entrust it to a single translator but to a diverse group. The editors of The Unsung Masters Series intuited that, to convey the texture of such a broad and varied work, multiple readings and sensitivities were required. A single voice risked flattening what in Cárdenas is heterogeneous. That is, his movement between lyric and narrative, between the intimate and the collective, between the urban and the Patagonian wind barren landscapes.

By chance—and by affinity—this translation team reproduced the typology cited by Juan G. Ramírez Giraldo[8] (drawing on Lesser). Within this framework, poets such as July Westhale, Julia Guez, and Mathew Weitman can be situated in the category of those who understand translation

[8] Ramírez Giraldo, Juan G. "The Limits and Forms of Literary Translation." *The Routledge Handbook of Literary Translation,* edited by Lawrence Raw, Routledge, 2018, pp. 61 – 77.

as a creative exercise; alongside them, a professional translator (María Paz Wallffiguer Mardones) brings rigor, thoroughness, and ethics; a bilingual lover of literature whose main occupation lies in other fields (Mary Ann Christensen) approaches translation from her own unique perspective; and academics, including Mathew and myself, turn to theory and criticism to look for answers.

This plurality becomes evident in the translators' notes: Julia Guez reflects on how to transform similes into metaphors to preserve the music of Spanish; Mary Ann Christensen focuses on maintaining rhythm and atmosphere, even if it means leaving words in Spanish or relying on family memory to name birds and trees; María Paz emphasizes the ethics of translation as a "labor of fatigue," where exhaustion is inseparable from responsibility; while I myself tend to read these decisions through literary theory, seeking the conceptual framework that helps us understand translation as a political and survivalist act.

As Westhale and Weitman underscore in their editorial notes, however, this project rests not only on the diversity of its translators but also on a community of affections surrounding Cárdenas's work. Jorge Aravena Llanca, his close friend, shared photographs and letters immediately and eagerly right after the first time we asked; Ramón Díaz Eterovic, who compiled the *Obra Completa*, transmitted his enthusiasm and granted permissions for use of his materials; Leonora Vicuña provided images of the poet; and María Cecilia Ojeda Cárdenas, the poet's niece, granted the legal authorization necessary for translation without further ado. Each contributed to an archive that is a collection of documents as well as a tapestry of shared memories and love.

This fabric of friendships and collaborations reminded me of Roberto Esposito's[9] reflection on community and melancholy. Around Cárdenas's work, a community has formed not through abundance or presence but through what is missed and absence: the absence of accessible editions, the absence of recognition in his own language, the absence of justice toward his poetry. Also through the melancholy that permeates his work, that austral solitude that is not only individual but also historical and collective. Translating him today is thus an act of repair inscribed within that same communal logic, a community that recognizes itself in that absence but transforms that into the energy to keep a voice alive.

In this sense, the editorial project is not simply the sum of translations; it is the consolidation of a network of affections and memories that prolongs Cárdenas's life beyond death and oblivion. As Díaz Eterovic remarked in a message: *"Me alegra saber que conoces la poesía de este poeta tan gigante, importante y desaparecido; me alegra más que trabajes en la traducción de sus poemas."*

* * *

Cárdenas and Comparatist Translation

TO SITUATE ROLANDO CÁRDENAS in English translation is to ask what place he occupies within the broader map of Chilean literature in translation. Gabriela Mistral, Nobel Prize winner, has been the object of multiple versions in English and other languages, though not without tensions. It is very likely that her work has been at times domesticated to fit international canons, at the cost of diluting its cultural specificity.

---

[9] Esposito, Roberto. "Melancolía y comunidad." *Comunidad: inmunidad y biopolítica*, Herder, 2009, pp. 141-154.

Cárdenas, by contrast, arrives at translation from a double periphery: geographical (Magallanes, at the far southern edge of the continent) and political (a poet whose works became nearly unfindable due to censorship and editorial precariousness). Translating him today is not simply adding another name to the list of Chilean authors in English but opening a comparative dialogue that questions the logic of canonization.

As Westhale and Weitman point out in their notes, Cárdenas's absence from circulation is not accidental but the product of historical and editorial processes that relegated him to the margins. From that testimonial observation, I propose an additional step: to figure his translation within a sort of reparative comparatism, one that does not compare centers to centers but instead relates peripheries, silences, and absences. His poetry of Magellanic exposure becomes a necessary counterpoint to more legitimized voices of the Chilean canon. In dialogue with Mistral or Teillier, Cárdenas represents a poetics of what is missing, yet essential.

Faced with the oblivion that ensnared him—due to editorial, historical, and geographical reasons—translation offers the possibility of prolonging his voice, of giving him a second life in another language. Following Benjamin, every translation extends a text's life, albeit provisionally. Following Derrida, that survival is never closure but infinite iteration. Following Spivak and Appiah, that prolongation must be ethical, respecting opacity, thickening context, resisting the erasure of difference.

But beyond theory, what makes this project urgent is the network of affections that sustains it. Friends, heirs, colleagues, translators, and readers have formed a community bound by absence, and it is from that absence that Cárdenas becomes present. Translating him today prolongs that community, registers his voice into a new map, and offers him the dignity denied in life and in his original language. It is not about inserting Cárdenas into a global canon devoid of tensions but about recognizing him in his southern singularity and allowing him to dialogue with others through difference.

From left to right: Jorge Aravena Llanca, Jorge Teillier, and Rolando Cárdenas at Gabriela Mistral's grave.

Rolando Cárdenas Biographical Timeline

March 23, 1933	Born in Punta Arenas
1940	Father dies Mother dies
Late 1940's – early 50's	Attends Escuela Superior de Hombres No. 15 Attends Armando Quezada Acharán industrial school Works as a laborer for the National Petroleum company
1954	Arrives in Santiago
Mid-1950's	Studies civil engineering at State Technical University Meets Jorge Teillier
1958	Wins Young Communists of the University of Chile poetry contest Publishes first poems in literary magazines
1959	*Tránsito Breve* wins Federación de Estudiantes de Chile (FECH) poetry contest
Early-1960's	Frequents Sociedad de Escritores de Chile (SECH)
1960	*En el Invierno de la Provincia* wins SECH poetry contest
1961	*Transito Breve* published

1963	*En el Invierno de la Provincia* published
1964	Meets Jorge Aravena Llanca *Personajes de Mi Ciudad* published
1965	Miller Williams translates three of Cárdenas's poems into English Attends Armando Quezada Acharán industrial school
1966	"Antepasados" anthologized in *The Best Chilean Poems*
Early-1970's	Becomes an active member of Chilean Communist Party Anthologized in *Chilean Poetry of the 20th Century* Anthologized in *Best 100 Chilean Poems* Anthologized in *Heroic Vietnam*
1970	Salvador Allende elected
1972	*Poemas Migratorios* wins Pedro de Oña Award
September 11, 1973	Military Coup Incarcerated in Estadio Chile for communist ties Dismissed from job
1974	Self-publishes *Poemas Migratorios*
Early 1980's	Frequents La Unión Chica Bar with fellow poets Meets Ramón Díaz Eterovic

1982	Returns to Punta Arenas for the last time
1986	*Que, Tras Esos Muros* published
1990	Eliana Oyarzo, Cárdenas's partner of twenty years, dies
October 17, 1990	Cárdenas dies in Santiago
1994	*Obra Completa* posthumously published

When It Is the Countryside We Are Searching For

Jorge Aravena Llanca, in Conversation with Felipe Acevedo Riquelme.

Translated by Daniela Anaís Jara Guevara and Valentina Merino Amigo. Berlin, Germany, 17 October 2024.

I MET ROLANDO CÁRDENAS—"el Chico" as everyone affectionately called him—one afternoon in June, 1964. I had just arrived in Santiago from Buenos Aires, where I'd lived for over 30 years. I was born in Santiago, but my mother, recently widowed and with five children, left our homeland and moved us to the Chilean embassy in Buenos Aires where her sister worked.

As an adult, I'd resolved to try to recover my Chilean nationality, which brought me back to Santiago. And this is how I met Rolando—one day in 1964, I decided to sit and rest in a restaurant called Full Bar on Bernardo O'Higgins Avenue, across from the Iglesia de San Francisco.[10] I was carrying my

[10] Historic church in Santiago

guitar slung over my back, and two cameras hanging from my neck: a Hasselblad 6x4 and a Contaflex 35mm. I saw a table with a few empty chairs where two young men were sitting before a bottle of white wine. Since the whole room was full, I asked them if I could sit at their table.

One of them was dark-skinned, very thin, with slicked-back hair; it was Rolando Cárdenas Vera, stretching out his hand. The other man introduced himself, his smile revealing a space where two front teeth once were—it was Jorge Teillier. Rolando, who spoke with his mouth wide open, revealed his uvula and vocal cords and the dark cave of his face, where nearly all his front teeth too were missing. He did not try to hide them.

"And who are you?" they asked me, almost in unison. I quickly learned they were both poets. Rolando showed interest in my guitar, so he asked me if he could have a look at it. He held it in his arms and strummed a precise and sonorous arpeggio. It brought me great joy, realizing this chance encounter between artists. Silently, Teillier gave me a look that I immediately knew meant he wanted to touch my cameras. I let him. Later, I found out that Teillier was someone who people used to talk about in the Chilean literary circle as one of the most promising poets of the Generation of 1950, to which Rolando also belonged.

Almost immediately after I introduced myself, they said: "You are Argentinian, *Che*![11] What are you doing around here? And so careless, carrying those two highly desired gadgets by the petty thieves and pickpockets that come into this bar?" We passed the time, ordered two bottles of Santa Carolina Tres Estrellas wine—drunk quickly—and we started to get to know one another. Again, I was joyful. I had always

[11] Hey

known that poets and musicians are mankind's best friends in every corner of the world.

It seemed to me that Jorge had a destiny, someone in a great literary story, or a tango song. Rolando, however, was a pure Chilean southerner; his impeccability would never betray what his poems did: that he was an ancestor of many who suffered greatly from European colonization, and the exploitation of his land of snowfalls, horses, and cold. The identity of full-time loneliness.

I'd had the thought, in that moment, of Omar Khayyam, and his lines about friendship and poetry and wine. And as if he's read my mind, Rolando looked at me and shouted: "'Wine! Hear my jokes! Red wine! Melodies of lute!' *¡Che, pibe!*[12] 'Thou who art a ghost, hide your distress because not everyone notices it!'" (trans.)[13]

He kept going. "Oh thou, who didst with pitfall and with gin beset the road I was to wander in."[14]

Above his recitation, his dark eyes: "You are the one who with pitfall and with gin beset the road I was to wander in!" (trans.)[15]

Then, a battle cry: "*Che*, Argentinian! 'Wretched are those who get caught in your devices for not avoiding their faces!'" (trans.)[16] What a way to introduce yourself!

---

[12] Boy

[13] Omar Khayyam's verses. Original: "¡Vino! ¡Escucha mis bromas! ¡Vinos rosas, cantos de laúd! ¡Che pibe, tú que eres un aparecido, disimula tu tristeza que no todos la advierten!"

[14] From "The Rubaiyat" translated by Edward FitzGerald, 1859.

[15] See footnote 10. Original: "Tú eres el que ha puesto trampas en todos los caminos que pretendes que sigamos."

[16] See footnote 10. Original: "Desdichados con tus aparatos para aquellos que no eviten sus rostros."

This was the first, intense, surprising thing about Rolando. I never thought my baptism back into Chilean would happen in such serene, thirsty, and auspicious circumstances.

These distant visions still live in my memory, sometimes like the cry of an old wound that hurts as much as being lost in the middle of the countryside, when it is the countryside itself that we are searching for. I learned to love Rolando like an older brother. He taught me to be the same kind of Chilean he was: purely of the people.

Brief Transits, 1961

Translated by July Westhale

Epitaph for an Infant

Now that the rain has unhidden everything
and gallops fragrantly over the night and sidewalks
it is useless to retain this solitary quiet
where mourning does not exist
nor good hopefulness
nor, either, the secret annihilation
of keeping fistfuls of pointed stars in our hands forever.

Almost nothing is revealed, only the rain
which on this night runs roots into the earth
and over the shrub rose sprouted with birds
in a manner both sweet and vague
like old legends of infancy.
Without knowing entirely, it is very certain that the night is outside
in her presence of lonely water,
and the silence like a smell
that smells the same as joy,
like everything now that grief does not exist,
nor good hopefulness,
nor, at least, the letter that tells us of other things, from other
latitudes.

The Search

At times it is good to abandon oneself in what is forgotten
as if knowing how to smile
were as easy as biting into fruit.
To go through the streets perfectly alone
without more company than our quotidian sadness, and our own
paths
loving at once the simplicity of air
which feels like childhood,
or other pulverized time
when we looked for the first stars in a pond.

It is good to sit amongst friends and glasses
and observe how everyone abandons something of themselves
in the music that impulsively transforms into boneless rhythms
while the night taps the walls
looking also for a place to hide her hopes,
and after, leaves towards the shrub roses
with a little more to feel future loneliness.

It is good to understand that we are made of memory,
that time grows without listening to us.
That there are many things we do not understand.

At times, it is good to hold oneself hostage in contemplating that
the leaf that falls
with the word "Spring"
is not what we would ever want it to be.

The Everyday Man

There is a daily gesture that tells us:
a certain mode of being will always denounce us,
and always time reminds us who we are.

Time was born one morning, soaked in roses,
after recounting remote birth,
after returning to school,
eating an orange slowly,
without concerning itself much with bridges,
without seeing how scarcely the countryside is drawn.

We take off our masks of sleep
to penetrate the day. Suddenly we remember
there are things to say
of no importance,
suddenly we copy attitudes as if in front of a mirror,
implacably, to be again ghosts between ghosts.

Therefore our grief remembers us
that once we could wound the day with a cry,
to hurl to ruins this slow death,
shorter than light on water.
That we can free ourselves from our lineages
that proceed tiredly from era to era,
that one can resuscitate the rain between the rocks.
Always our forgetfulness,
without the need to wait for the stars
to search the dictionary for the word *lost*.

The Night Hour

While I drink this coffee made of small sips
I go for my memories like an echo—
this night of hours grinding into themselves
without making a single sound,
as it the night itself were very slight
and the leaf's falling means nothing to no one,
least of all to you
that you read reclined in the stars
without repairing my recollections.

The silence tells me I am the owner of voice
and that your presence, unique and beloved,
that you knew. You move less painfully through this
 tight reality.
But nothing reveals to me your existence
aside from the water that illuminates your eyes.
Your breath calls me from anxiety,
your hands recuperate the caress.

There is nothing that defines this nightly turn
as tranquil but the softest light,
or the call of the air, which is now still.

Adrift, in the lurch, I go for my thoughts,
feeling how the night pulls them to sleep
but quiet and alone
as to not disturb your calm abandonment
but rather to recover it a little,
in this rapturous hour
something of your old presence,

different now than what tremors in my chest.
I return to be, then
the same who strokes your adolescent memory,
        extinguished in idle hours.

From Now On I Love You

For M.M.

From now on I love you,
and you haven't been the same since.
My crude hands have molded you
pure clay with black eyes
giving you rain-form and my youth
and the suave sadness that was mine before you.

You came from the South,
from southern shrubs with their rumors of markets,
you smelled of villages,
your soaked body
from the tranquil rains of your beloved Chillan.

You have not been the same
since the minute my words
fell drop by drop on your silence,
spilled from my starred dreams.

O, my bell-heart,
you make time's fall more slight
for this tender fugitive
for the sadness of hope abandoned—such heaven.

What does it matter the name I give you?
You are all memory,
sweeter than the light of stars.
At times, I fall silent to hear you laugh.
You are the musical urn that encases your simplicity.

Maybe I love you for this,
because you are like my village
situated at the most southern point in the universe.

O, owner of this hallucinated countryside,
presence and message of blue rain,
absolutely fragrant of your held-dear Chillan.

Posthumous Memory of My Mother

I do not remember her likeness,
having known her very little, hardly at all,
in my dirty years of my infancy's earth.

I evoke her in a spinning top that does not turn.
In ships, in houses, in the first doves
she taught me to draw in notebooks,
which I was daily inclined to do, after the stupor
of sobs, the most perfect science.

She was the mistress of the shrub rose, the risen night.
Her dew-enclosed song between the house's walls
that still lifts the ghost between wind and snow.
Their passage revives the items in the rooms,
even the simplest events, highlighted
in the jingle of the pots.
My childhood, guided wisely by her hand,
had thereafter the bittersweet flavor of a ripe apple.
She departed one Spring, and all other Springs
were still the same imperturbable sweetness,
only finely fogged over with her presence.

How I remember, too,
soft sadness in a drawn smile,
as imperceptible as a sudden blaze,
She was grieving. A grief like slow rain
over temple roofs—a grief
that wounds all the correct words.

I began to love her deep tenderness,
the same that brought me to the world with purest stroke.
And to mourn autumn, or winter, indefinitely gone.

Since this day, recently verified,
she has been ghostly vigilant of my bread
and the bread of all my young siblings.
She, an interrupted dream,
saves us sun's sweetest hours—
Aprils, rains—
that quench the trees in the Patagonian earth.

For this perhaps I ignored my mother,
her intact laugh,
the tranquil love of her hands
washed in the green Chilote archipelago.
For this perhaps she smelled of song,
a precise water whose murmur
penetrates the sown fields. It was these small,
small blue villages that were made in the times of stars.
She wanders the twilight,
the silent, transparent ears of corn.

When my father marched with his yield,
lifting them with severe gusto
on his horse in the callous manner of countrymen,
a secret happiness swung in the winds.
The sunsets jokingly went down gray,
discoloring things, blurring their outlines.
Sundays were for the songs

of some rooster. In the winter nights,
hatefully long, beside the fire
that consumed the hours and the wood,
my mother read to me.
This struck, for me, the timorous shadows
on the wide horizons of this enchanted country.
Slitting the throats of giants, killing myself with stars and
solitude.

Time blooms. One makes due with the bell.
Swallows grow to the sky,
looking for their lost reflections in that great mirror.
Always her presence, lighting up the water
in a wise, exact way, like the seasons.

Still, one day silence came to get her.
It took her hopefully, dreamy soul.
I saw it this afternoon, with her accompanying grief
of slow fog, her light smile,
her incomplete tenderness. I did not understand a thing.
I only felt a species of quiet shadow,
mystery. All these years
the winter does a little march of the flowers it covers.

Tell Me

Tell me, little one,
in this unreachable and solo hour
that stretches itself until it is countryside,
something of what I have forgotten,
or of this new, growing solitude.

Tell me,
before the afternoon falls between hours,
or before your words become soft moss,
that your voice will own me, force silence.

Tell me.
I listen to you from here,
from the jungle-smelling table,
from the remembered, momentary things,
from lonely hours climbing up like creepers.

Now that I have born this antique love
I hardly breathe, to keep your words.

Tell me, little
wounded rainstorm, beloved fondness,
wild and savage and lost ache, throughout the years,
tell me all, something. Nothing.
Tell me.

Interior

"Tell me you love me greatly,"
you say, lounging in the afternoon
but with a clear, morning smile.
It falls from your hands, makes love in your voice.
It rebounds off all around you.
It is as if you elevate all touched by your soul—
As if love's protest spent far too long locked up.
You shake in the words.

You say you love me greatly
and I like how you say it.
It is like the green underside of a leaf
that goes running in Autumn
towards the country where flight does not exist,
towards the ecstatic mouth
which awaits the return of night's blossom.

You say it as such:
you love me *greatly*
your voice plays kissingly as you speak.
I take your words between my arms,
quaking, maybe, though I cannot be certain.
The bittersweet salves future absence. Maybe.

You made a habit of arriving in tense hope,
soaked in *adios*,
in a new dress for a new party,
ready with calm palms, a calm caress,
like clusters of ready fruit,
flapping wings, new also, at your throat.
They spill like water over my thick silence.

This is where your love lives—
saved in my book like a dried leaf.
When you speak it like you speak it,
time unmakes all lived hours.

I've never archived your many sayings,
which have at times brought me to laughter.
Your ease impacts all.
I only know they were true,
so true, as true as the present,
until the hour becomes overtaken with oblivion.

When your voice is the wind
and tells me of great love
I should have saved it all, and its echo,
in time's book, with my dried leaves.

O, voice of the past, beloved, which abandons me in this future—
you are unmade by farewell.

Retrospective

Until recently, I collected
love's mouth as though it was mine,
as naturally as one drinks
a glass of bracing water.

We call this sadness as if it was
something necessary, filling
hands and eyes with double-edged cries,
making it more complete
than plentitude in the same measure.

You are now someone different,
because the reality of you stayed
in Spring. The astonishment is a dream
never recovered. It is Autumn now,
the time of diluted chimes, of joy
that hasn't yet been heightened.
I flash suddenly: your shadow dance,
insane with wine, a strange possibility
that never dies but is always resuscitated
orgiastically, more bitter than an inexhaustible memory.

For all the blueness you created, I stayed
in the daily anxiousness, hungover
on the caresses of different hours.
You never said: "There is still time to keep this heaven intact."

I walked, searching for the nerve of my own life,
searching for the exit of my own exile,
falling down in abandonment after abandonment,
unknowingly killing myself, rebellious

and excessive, permitting my soul
to become accustomed to absence.
If I found my nerve, you'd destroy its purest
call, shatter the dream with dawn, a dream
realized a dream, all in the same way
wings know how to flap without disturbing
a body much, as if you believed
the first scent of heaven would return
and renew us all.

It is impossible to find you like before,
even in searching my memory. Perhaps
for this reason, I momentarily forget. I cannot
situate you there or me there,
precisely now, when I most need
the lucid word that would help me
escape the lost dream, would help me
penetrate your deepest and most unknown
actions, would help me search for a light
for all the time spent quietly wounded.

Autumn escapes in leaves. I don't know
if it's too late for new death or renewal.
I just know my sadness, which lights up
when, from the depths of photos, you smile
at me as if it were Spring.

This image persists, almost unreal in presence,
despite time tending its own tortured face.
My solitude newly calls you,
like something necessary and everyday.

Elegy of a Future Suicide

I speak of integrity as if the word itself were indivisible,
or as if everything would ever return to nothing.

It's not like that.

There comes a time when the dream ends.
The hand no longer wants to imprison.
The flower forgets its plumage among the moss.
Eyes stay dry.
Caresses don't exist.
Nor a loving word.
Nor a rumor that can bring back the leafy willow forest.

It matters not that the wind bangs in every door frame.
That the rain dampens our shoes and our souls.
That apathy is a vulture that slits hope to pieces.

You want to trap a laugh in a fist, like a butterfly
but it moves towards away. It doesn't want to share
the kiss the mouth will deliver absently,
nor the body that gives in furtive hours,
nor the word driven to conquer the air.

Loneliness grows, an indefatigable plant,
building a garden of smiling mourners.
Memory lies demolished by asthenia, delirious,
incapable even of creating a wilderness of anguish.

Indifference pierces the skin. It gnaws a little.
It's astonishing. We didn't believe the grief

that signaled to us our own miserable resignation.
Joy has been long knocked into some nook
of our own forgetting.

The tongue doesn't blaspheme.
It is ecstatic and alone.
Alongside it, the truncated song
that once proclaimed strength.

The heart continues on alone—
during the day, at night, abandoned
as anguish.

Nothing is too indispensable. Just air.
Fatigue forges its own tears,
everything beat back quickly
to the end. In the hardest hour,
nothing stays: purity, love's
light-filled time, all
painful in their inexistence.

The end of time comes, awaiting
us like an insurmountable wall.
That it is bare is just another way
of demonstrating its certainty.

One can also laugh at the border of life.

I Only Know That I Keep Going Back

Never was my sadness more quiet and calm
than my memory of you: always
a conjunction of principles.

I would never have the tranquil disposition
my mother had. I'm a specter who wears
my own clothing, speaks my own words
while searching for an ear, hesitant. It just
can't be any other way. Dawn enters
as if through a door, and finds me alone
until the next dawn. Finds too my books,
some more precious than others, waiting
quietly to be infiltrated by a studious eye,
that showed me the enchanted world of things.

I return now to the same hours that once carried me
by hand through my placid infancy. There
I encountered them as if they never existed.
Yet there is my friend the street, there is the same
street hunched over by rain and snow, farther
over there is my ancient friend the ocean,
who caresses eternally this tranquil city,
there are the faraway hills, and the wind's flute
playing over sidewalks, the friendly faces,
the hands and mouths that smile
after so much time away.

But it's not possible.
I only know I am a little sad, a little exhausted
of dreaming so frequently of the twilight

I touch now with my hands.
I wanted to tell you something different.
Searching for something different, I sailed
this afternoon on my dreams and memories like a ship.

I always want to enter things
to understand how they are the way they are,
including water's simple song. But when I converse
with my hands, I can't help but be more hushed,
a manifestation of my grief, as I am never sure of anything.
Not even my existence in this blue afternoon,
not even that you are beside me
with all the quietude of a bloom. Of nothing I am certain.
I confess. It was that, precisely that which was there
before I saw you, that I wanted to talk to you about . . .
but now it is late. There is a lot of sun.
Maybe tomorrow the dawn will tell you . . .

Epilogue

I wanted to die one blue afternoon,
languishing in my books alone.
It could be far from my familiar house
in an unknown city.
It could also be the mountains,
close to the sea, or whichever place pleases,
but if nothing else, I am told I once was loved,
even if just the tenacious love of my mother.
I am certain I was alive
when I screamed my first scream,
when the light was mine.

Maybe they will say and think many things
after I have retired to the destroyed hour,
perhaps, but it will be late then.
Someone will speak to my virtues.
Others, my defects.
Then they will think I lacked the valor to face the world—
but they will be mistaken,
and for that I will remain
profoundly mute,
without defending an unfathomable minute of it.

In this, everything matters, including the outpouring of sorrow.
After, everything will continue as before.
This is the way of things.

I will go slowly, my last night,
always as quiet and alone as my books, how I was in life.
Perhaps a little pain,

because I lived to be loved,
and its scent left without ever touching me.

Of course I would not have had the things I had—
For example, my first kite,
in which my childhood dreams sung,
or the contented weeping
of crushing fruit between my fingers.

Not even if I had the escape
of the sun, the perforated night,
nor the song of my feet on paths
about the crystalized ground of my village,
nor the mosaic of countrysides
that made up my joy—
in my dreamy state, horizontal and eternal,
I will look to the marvelous life of your mouth,
which you gave willingly to me,
and which smelled of new wood.

I will have nothing. And all will be the same.

No one can say if death will make me quieter. Or more joyful.
At times, the tenor of sorry
reaches the height of the sob.
In any case, I imagine peace,
wandering twilight,
think of and love you from other latitudes,
remembering the first pain,

the first joy,
the first words I slid into your ear's shell.

I will miss the free things:
our bodies together in arabesques
in the blue smell of cigarettes,
while our friends speak of far-off homelands
with their voices and souls humid
like the fog that slips to the backs of vases,
the parties, the songs,
the verses said in the dead of the afternoon,
the chain of familiars,
until the furtive kiss, given by the mouth to the soul.

Top row, left to right: Raul Mellado, Jorge Teillier, Unknown, Omar Lara, Waldo Rojas, Unknown, Unknown; Bottom row, left to right: Ronnie Muñoz, Rolando Cárdenas, Rolando Gabrielli, Ariel Peralta.

*From left to right: Rolando Cárdenas, Jorge Arevena Llanca,
Samuel Donoso, Jorge Teillier.*

Poems That Grow Lichen Over Time: On Translating *Brief Transits* and *Characters of My City*

July Westhale

As with the most impactful poetic works, the true artistry of Rolando Cárdenas is the ability to bring the sharpness and duality of a country under siege to light with stunning alacrity. In his time and retrospectively, he was well-known nationally as a writer of *la soledad magellanico*, or the specific solitude of the Magellan region. His work is infused with human generosity (and emotional complication), especially as it intersects with the natural world and the landscape of his own Punta Arenas.

I believe that literary translation is one of the deepest forms of intimacy a reader can have with a piece of writing. This feels particularly true with poetry, where the act of translation is not only content and form, but also the consideration of white space, which is to say, the very consideration of breath. I was fortunate enough to translate

Brief Transits and *Characters of My City* in their entirety, and several poems in *In the Winter of the Province*. While these are all markedly different collections, they are recognizably his work; they are so rich with blue humidity, snow, and moisture, the poems themselves seem to grow lichen over time. Those who loved the poet called him "the rain traveler," and we can understand why; in these poems are the deep acoustics of winter, the ghosts and ghost ships and dreams of those here and no longer here. It is difficult sometimes to discern which and whom are what and where, and this is by design. The prose-like paragraphs that make up the poems in *Characters of My City*, while full of the characteristicly observant nature we have come to expect from him, offer a more concrete study than we typically see from the poet: archetypes of people, presented solidly, even more solid-seeming against the specter-like backdrop of place.

A note on my own translation and process: I heavily consulted with friends, archives, and the footnotes in the Chilean National Library for context outside of my sphere of cultural knowledge (names of birds from Punta Arenas, a few instances of bygone slang, and when navigating the extremely varied—and often under-discussed—folklore of Chiloé). Additionally, the convergence of all translators working on *In the Winter of the Province* offers the sort of textured dinner conversation that can only happen when translations are juxtaposed next to one another.

Landscape, Community, and Subjectivity: *poesía lárica* as Suspension in the Work of Rolando Cárdenas and Jorge Teillier

Biviana Hernández

"The earth passes with its old crust
damp and alone, like the first time."
—Rolando Cárdenas

LIKE RIGOROUS AND SLOW MOSS growing as a silent circle of hard waters and secret roots: this is how Rolando Cárdenas (1933 – 1990) imagined the southernmost region of Chile. Like a vast heart of solitudes where, whispering, the stories of blood and ghosts still throb in poetic veins.

It is impossible not to link the life and work of the Magellanic writer with Chilean *poesía lárica*; a tendency usually circumscribed to the literary production of Jorge Teillier, as if the vocative "lárico" had been co-opted by the (authorial) authority of his name. Still, it is undeniable the strength of the many other voices that also delved into the aesthetics of landscapes and their affective-imaginative relation with myth, history, and childhood within the framework of the literary generations of the 1950s and 1960s in Chile and later—I am thinking, for example, of Efraín Barquero or Delia Domínguez.

The emergence of the collective *Pueblos Abandonados*[17], to mention a recent case, serves as a reference to illustrate the validity that the *lárica* tradition still has today among new offsprings of provincial writers, or those who make of it a representational enclave to continue imagining the links between landscape, community, and subjectivity.

At the same time, it is also indisputable that the writing of Rolando Cárdenas seems to have remained suspended along with the solitary *pampas*, the blizzards, and the freezing rains, through which the geography of his poetry overflows. That is a word that manages to harmonize the *lárica* motifs—the topography of his own habitat, the ways of life of the Magellanic inhabitant, the history of its founders—with the emotional disposition of a subject inclined to solitude, melancholy, and disquiet in the face of a time which, impenetrable, passes toward nothingness, loss, or emptiness, but does not yield before the memory of its origins. That is why, in his verses, the *topos* of the house, the neighborhood streets, friends, parents, and grandparents coexist with that of the trees, the sea, the snow, and the frost, "rough edges" of the South that resist the finitude of human existence or the hostility of the environment. So much so that the return—suffused with memory—to those physical, mental, and symbolic landscapes is what makes it possible to transcend temporality and, with it, the finitude of things and people loved by the poet.

In his collection, *In the Winter of the Province*, lies the poetic terroir of Rolando Cárdenas via his native soil: Magallanes. It highlights the physiognomy of the austral

[17] The Pueblos Abandonados collective gathers authors from several regions of Chile; among them, Oscar Barrientos, Cristian Geisse, Cristóbal Gaete, Mario Verdugo and Marcelo Mellado.
For more information (in Spanish), see:
http://letras.mysite.com/mme090413.html

landscape and, with exacerbated latency, the desire to elevate the concepts of family and home to the condition of myth, as happens with the figures of the grandparents in the peom "Weaving Hands:"

> This is how I knew her:
> bent over warp & weft
> as if lighting a fire
> or setting a table—
> her tireless hands
> weaving vigils
> with stars & wind.

This is also present in "The Country House":

> My grandfather grew old with this land.
> He was a watchman of orchards
> and crops, up before the dew
> with his shovel and his cigar,
> warming the earth with his conversation,
> protecting it from grand frosts.

The images elaborated in these verses sketch the mythical dimension of the archaic societies to which they allude, that is, the sacred ritual of sowings and harvests in the eternal return of their permanence. Hence in his poetry the return to the village constitutes an aesthetic and vital act always positive and joyful; a physical but also mythical return to that frosted city where the encounter with ancestors grants the subject the gift of vision and of the word:

> One day, we will return to the lost city
> —like the seasons to a year

or shadows to the afternoon—
& ask about our ancestors
& the river, whose waters
broke the sky.

The poem "Return" is paradigmatic in this sense, insofar as the subject who returns to his native city is not a stranger, or rather, does not perceive himself as someone alien, unawaited. On the contrary, he feels happy with the idea of returning to the same places and of knowing that there will always be someone to recognize him "at every turn around the corner". Thus, although time has passed, taking with it many of his loved ones,

The bar
where old workers gathered
still exists—
[. . .]
& we'll say hello
from another era.

The poetic voice of Cárdenas trusts in the survival of the tavern or of the table where he will sit to taste the bread of other days and to converse, perhaps with new patrons, "unspoken subjects / no one could forget." The enduring, the transcendent is found in the small rituals summoned by the affective presence of the truly beloved. In this lies the primordial matter of the *lárico* poet: situated in the land, that vast heart of solitudes that is Magallanes becomes impregnated with life and with a telluric force that imprints on its inhabitant the essence of his world. A poetic, emotional, sentimental world, for which the sea, the wind, and the snow ceaselessly reconstruct the memory that shakes from its roots.

In the Winter of the Province, 1963

Translated by Julia Guez, July Westhale, Miller Williams, Mathew Weitman, María Paz Wallffiguer Mardones, Mary Ann Christensen, and Felipe Acevedo Riquelme

Message for Magallanes (From the Stone)

Translated by Julia Guez

The South I remember. I remember you,
the wild look of you and your stars,
your complete silence, a circle
growing like moss, that rigorous, that slow.
That's how I remember you,
made exactly what you are by so much hard water,
perfectly textured by these secret roots
criss-crossing a terrestrial sky.
Something to do with you,
the hard wood of your forests,
the fiber, the fragrance
lingering in your big heart whose lonelinesses
ships and cities come from.
And the wind, only the wind
could care less and gallops on
carrying gruesome ghost stories, full of blood and gore.
The persistence of rain, ever present rain
dances alone, at first, then floods the air.
South of winter, the snow there always
repeats itself, inexhaustible and alone.
In my retinas, I reconstruct
the contours of your light, and your snowstorms,
and for people who've only known sun,
I give them your geography, piece by piece.
With a fistful of snow in my hands
and this wild wind in my hair,
I tell them I come from your rough edges.

That plows are distressed by your cold hard ground.
That the sky is an immense belltower
where birds and hail gather.
That there are reefs made by sea-foam
where the sea spits, the sea howls
and pirates who couldn't fathom
your waters are made to lie on the moon.
That sometimes your most remote fields tremble
at the sound of a sheepdog, when a herd of sheep passes by,
where planets dream along with the dawn
listening to the tunes rain and memory play on.
That where I come close to your wide open window
to see the birds, the landscape fills the frame to brimming.

That's how I remember you,
a damp sail,
adding even deeper silence to the stone,
so it seems more intact somehow among the algae and the ice-cold meridians.
Ever since a million water-drops rose up to form the sea
everything here's been ready for oblivion.

Nothing's been left out, not the runaway sun or season,
not the rocks and the channels, the complicated pattern they form,
not even your jutting architecture, made out of horizons alone,
not the sky you'll leave behind,
not the fog, enemy of light.

There you'll stay, falling off the map,
molding the rough clay of my childhood,
maintaining your distance, as if it were an air,
an attitude, one of always waiting for the swallows.

That's how I remember you,
this unnecessary gift from the sun.

Wharves

Translated by Miller Williams

Again the goodbyes.
Someone has left the customary words
forgotten on the wood and the iron.
The wharves, with their gulls and the great derricks,
might also leave.

A black smoke rises and the water turns dark.

A tepid summer falls on the last port.
Near the distant, battered wharves
rusty skeletons are shaken by the sea.
Time sticks roots in their sides.
By night the island legends are told again.
They come back, illuminated by the storm,
and like misshapen specters
sail the channels again.

A whistle and the gulls fly higher.
The morning, barely existing,
falls away like confused words.
When there are no contours left
and we can only see with our thoughts,
the Southern Cross
will light us through the strait.

Tierra del Fuego

Translated by Miller Williams

I have looked at it from the tricky mountains
of Brunswick Peninsula
and it seemed a great blue haze
as if evening were forming on the horizon.
If the old sailors of four centuries ago
were to return and sail this strait
they would still see blinking fires in the night
where the Indians busied themselves burning shrubs
to make the land fruitful again
or went hunting in their canoes
chopped out of trees.

Many times, since the roots have wakened from their
    dream,
the leaves of the oak have turned red
and the moon has changed its shape
while water and air grew hard.

The wind from the west would pass over
telling the lay of the land and the longitude of the
    Darwin,
of its smallest cliffs and coasts,
with an obscure pain.
Out of the bark came a white fog
like a beard or a heavy perfume
of recently opened earth in a punctual rain.

The sea is the grand encircling rampart
and there is no other sound more powerful—
no other wanton, no other single clamor

as when it shatters on the sheer rocks.
Underneath, the sea trembles majestically,
and the stars shimmer on the water.

The day pushes its four seasons forward,
wakes to seabirds screaming.
It has a face of stone,
or only white,
an ancient face rising from the red earth
before the sun and the moon
when its mountains were still great hunters.

The solitude never resting, blows upon it.
The sky grows, and never uncovers the mystery:
so the navigators saw it four centuries ago.

The fires draw together toward the south,
Toward where the night, or the day, endures
through the long months.

The Rain Traveler

Translated by July Westhale

A mature air trembles in the humid earth,
which still has traces of ancient winters.

Due to the June rains, rustlers stalk
the moon's complicit face. It is night.
Night and earth seem as such;
Both are full of rumors and secrets.

My father slept in it when fatigue
surprised him on the plains, with dreams
similar to those of the ocean,
like a fallen tree watched by dogs.

Now his shadow will once again travel
through the land, regions of another time,
along the Southern and Eastern coasts of the island,
to the Rio Grande. If he were alive, he'd have
surely gone out on his horse, like a ghost alone
under the sky, to count his stars,
to verify his darkness. He'd have stopped
to observe the seasons and their invariable
rebellious signs: "It will surely rain tomorrow
because the clouds have descended over the mountains."

In his dreams they will spread along
good roads like a slow and imprecise fog,
leaving no trace on the wet prairie grass.
On the lonely embarcaderos, old steamers
leave loaded with wood evening to evening,
or outdated tugboats return in gray mornings,

as in the gold rushes of the last century,
weighed down with legends of wolf catchers.

But a house located anywhere in Autumn
will be only a lamp for the rain traveler's shadow,
returning to rest.

The Legend of Winter

Translated by July Westhale

In the mists, in the first snowfall,
when the forests resembled
a grandfather's white beard
and the solitude was a quiet harbor
inhabited by sea birds, where the ice
rolled with the noise of high drifts,
there were vast lands at which
no one arrived, south
of the last latitude.

Everything occurred as if in a white dream.
The nights were transformed by stars,
but the days remained the same.
The winds pushed autumn's forgotten fog,
that appeared hovering over the sea,
as if mysteriously emerging from the air,
and frightened seagulls found refuge among rocks.

The islands wished to leave, thrust by winds,
to hide their sullen tenderness, to protect
their roots from the first corsairs
that touched their shores. They came from strange
Nordic cities, or ancient Atlantic countries.
They came from so far, just to witness
the islands' oceanic minerals, to witness
their literal ruin, to remain in their powerful
silence, interrupted only by storms,
and the eternal cries of seagulls.

They ventured through gulfs and estuaries
so the land would give them its most intimate secrets.
But winter was the protective hand,
the silent forests like cemeteries full of rituals
and nocturnal birds. Many were left in distant
Puerto Hambre, frozen in frost
under a merciless sky.

Later, new sailors arrived from the other side
of the ocean, hovering like birds of prey
around the taciturn natives, who were none the wiser.
These were the ones who got rich by stripping them
of their wolf or guanaco skins, trading for a few
colored pieces of glass, a bottle of grappa,
or a miserable piece of bread.

There is a light, like a broken sky, that precedes a storm.
It trembles for a moment in the Strait.
Somewhere on the coast that no one knows about,
a pirate galleon drops its anchors.

We know it is the wind's fault, and the confusing
light from the sky. Tomorrow everything
will be forgotten when the birds disrupt
the air, as always, and the faint sun
stops over the broken earth.

The Earth Passes

Translated by María Paz Wallffiguer Mardones

The earth of the night passes,
almost like a window that does not open
to the presence of rain.
The earth passes with its old crust
damp and alone, like the first time.
Its breath does not stop before this sleeping house.
It is a wind ruffling a black mane of hair.
And this endless earth has no eyes.
And it has no rest,
like the rivers that cut through it.
Those who first lived on it pass
turned into forests or hills,
and one day disappeared behind the planets.
My ancestors pass, moving in a breath.
They are the ones who always wander between water
and foliage.
This sky full of voices never stops growing,
this dark sky, hardened with secrets
that leaves its soft dream among us
and touches me with a hand of water.
Confused by sounds that never cease,
hidden beneath a thick sky in constant vigil,
the earth of the night passes
with its shadows
and the mysterious scent of its roots.

Fueguinos

Translated by María Paz Wallffiguer Mardones

The first men were made of dark clay
by an ancestor who lived in the sky.
They were always moving away
among rocky islets,
beyond Cape Froward
or along the far shores of the Beagle Channel,

where the seasons resemble one another.
They knew the icy wind that blew from the ocean
when the branches of bushes shook.
They waited for the first guanacos
to come down to the beaches, fleeing the snow
to provide themselves with their fur all winter.
From a hollow oak tree, canoes were born,
while the women
searched for birds' eggs in the spring,
"for in another season trees refuse."
There, where the story of a forest begins
and the thick curtain of rain
makes one believe it will rain forever,
from the silent tents.
They knew how to keep warm
by burning whole logs.
They stayed by its side as if sleepy,
because it was beautiful to see a huge tree burning,
writhing, red, in the middle of the wind and the night.
They never knew of death,
because they recovered time in the secret of water.
But they were moving away from the north
inside a hollow oak tree.
Now they are the rivers and the mountains,
the red stars that cross the night.

Ancestors

Translated by July Westhale

They were born there. In the small
wooden towns, before canals. All
with the attitudes of their own islands,
fragile and slender as boats. They were
born at the very edge of the sea,
where the flight of blue horizons begins
and the sound of their roots become confused.

They had no concern, other than the sea.
They always waited for the fisherman's return,
sargassum pressed in their blue fingers, and talked
of harvests, of the coming rains.

Many went like rivers towards lands
where fires burned throughout the night
and the icebergs and the mists
recreated ghost ships.

To the South they came with their spells
and their braziers, to establish the wonder
of their crops, their toasted flour, their seafood
soups, and their brown bread.

They were the same Chilotes
from the happy dungeon of Sundays,
who cut firewood in the mountains with their
powerful arms, who knew a storm was coming
because bees gathered before it, who arrived
with their simple chores when the south
was still a tight silence of stars and vigils,
and the trees bent in tragedy to the wind.

They arrived at a time when winter was tangled
in cliffs that longed to touch the sky,
when the strange shapes of the islands were undoubting,
sailing towards silent and solemn snowdrifts,
like great wandering ice.

They knew the enigma of wood and earth
when they migrated like birds from another season,
to the city almost lost in fog. They raised
their red roof in the midst of other red roofs,
though in winter they would all look the same.

Many hands have learned from their hands,
around them like a circle, and many more will inherit
their water, their clay. And some have stopped
as if to rest, for long years, where bonfires continue to burn all night.

Overend

Translated by July Westhale

There is nothing behind these rocks, behind
the origin that asks for eternity from a land
that does not exist. The perfect, painful air
does not rest, the loneliness comes like a river
from the heavens, distant and deep
like the flickering of planets.

Nothing, except to think about the lost routes
of ships searching for cities in thick mists,
which sometimes appeared through the rain,
or when the sun opened the horizon
and they shined like snow in the three waters of Paine.

The relentless sea is full of something human
and taciturn within its bay, surrounded by a red
and petrified crust, expressionless and powerful
like the dreams of those drowned far away from lighthouses.

Still, the oily matter of it softens when it copies
the flight of hundreds of petrels.

In the end, beyond what has not yet happened
and beyond what we do not know, everything
is older than silence, the night and the dark
birds are alike, there are cities of gold
where one never dies, there is water and rock
stained by moss, and a rain that, again and again,
constructs distances, in search of good land
that will make forests emerge.

The Roads Drift Away

Translated by Julia Guez

Roads drift away without a word,
like a quiet river in the country
whose water will never know summer, the dust of one.

City wants to get out
to villages that are still still.
That's the key. And we've always dreamed of finding
the magic key
to figuring out where we'd lost our way.

Roads stay put.
They really only wait for the seasons
to cross over them like a herd of young horses,
or ghosts of shepherds
buried in the snow
who roam around on unreal hooves.

Roads drift away.
A secret desire to leave remains.
All roads lead to night.
Like dreams, they diverge
south of here, beyond these skies,
where the land begins to forget, begins to break up
and only the air's intact and hardened.

Nights of My City

Translated by July Westhale

I.

A chilled bird in the Earth's last nook,
where the mysterious eternity
of ice comes, and nothing of day remains
but the traces of snow on rooftops,
owner of invisible silences
and absent springs.

When we walk, our footsteps penetrate
the mourning streets like ghosts,
and we look for the nook's faintest
light. We simply want to escape
to a tenderly distant time, and something
that is not exactly a song burns our throats
and is confused with sadness, almost
secretly. We remember the wine
and friendship of our friend
who waits for us with his simple
bird heart, and it is like a fire to us.
Remembering the loneliness
crowing to the sky like an upright rooster,
while outside a vague, almost-limitless fog
begs like a destitute man for just a few coins.

II.

Some dog moans at the shadows, even
though the sky does not exist. Some
body says tomorrow will be the same,
that they long for the slow blinks of summer.
For now, coffee is our steaming joy,

like the eyes of a girl whose name
we keep silent. Whose presence
the world wants to free us from.
The hard hooves of frost pressing stars
in the water. To not forget
the stories of the old rustlers
who speak to us with the slow voice
of the pampas, the wind hides itself,
scratching at the shed doors where no one
goes in search of firewood.

There is barely enough fire left
to warm the dreams of these words.
The lonely streets. The tired clock
on the table. The deserted rain.

Birds

Translated by Julia Guez

No trace of them, or their feet;
the landscape's not motionless anymore.

Invisible hills appear mid-air
like faraway cities re-appear, after fog has cleared.
Beyond their wings there's a dream
we can't shake
because it's a window to the night and it's open.

Not much has changed since then,
but at the house, on the patio,
the birds perch in a heaven-sent tree.
And the child we are seems
to have lost something,
even though the sweet-sounding sea
still surrounds the city like a huge wall.

The air has filled with circles.

On that path, the one from the other day,
the light is lost, when birds don't sing.

They'll stay hidden, until the instinct to tear into
into some other sky's lagoon sets in again.

Springs

Translated by July Westhale

Goodbyes reappear.
Someone left the usual words forgotten
along with the wood and iron.
The docks, too, want to march
with their seagulls, their huge cranes.

A black smoke darkens the water.

Summer falls warmly on the last port.
Farther down, by the broken docks, lie
rusty ships tumbled by the thick sea.
Time takes root on their sides. These island
legends are repeated at night, rising
illuminated under the storm like strange
deformed spectators as they
navigate the channels again and again.

Whistling, the gulls fly higher.
The ghost ship barely existed this morning,
moving away like confused words.
When there are no contours left
and only our thoughts still see them,
the Southern Cross will overshadow
the path of the Strait.

We Listen to it Rain

Translated by Julia Guez

—for León Ocqeteaux

We listen to the rain,
the lugubrious sound of the wind;
together they make the sky's outer districts all but disappear.

The sun's pulled away from the poor corners
on the patio.
The sun has fled like frightened birds
trying to find a door.

Nothing interrupts the silence of this house, or its sullenness.
The cat's found refuge, under the stove.
The same rain pelting these windows,
cutting deep ruts in the earth
outside, it speaks.

We listen to the rain as we have listened to the rain for years.
Nothing has really changed:
not the glasses, not the table,
not the wind gusts or the walls, the way they shudder.

Like peals of thunder lost in the hills,
words lose their way.
The day ends. Streets are alone
with specters of mansions in ruins.

Tomorrow a sweet mist will rise up from the earth,
and, forgotten in the puddles, only the tired
image of the sky will be what's left.

The Reunited Family

Translated by María Paz Wallffiguer Mardones

It was the table with its deep profound,
ancient as its bread or its wine,
with its everyday white face,
with the same gestures and the same words,
as if it were water or a door.
It was time pausing to scrutinize
and it went unnoticed because it always repeated itself,
except for the snow that reappeared

and sat at it like every winter.
Many times they secretly rejuvenated,
other times, they had the maturity of the earth,
yet it was almost an unchanging attitude,
a rest, to see them once more,
although tenderness was hazily the same
and only death astonished them.
They were among each other like an old custom
and chatted on the last shore of the years,
perfectly calm from so far away
by the table or the window
listening to the fragile songs of a downpour,
without fears, expecting little,
like the day before.

Weaving Hands

Translated by Mathew Weitman

Hunched tenderly over her spindle,
my grandmother's hands are like old wood.

Silent as a tree at night, she is a fixture
of the house, thinning dark wool
the way I read long letters.
Maybe it is their manner of resting—
as if she followed each familiar thread
back to the wheatfields
of a shepherd's autumnal home.

Her hands are like a nest of chicks
as she kneels on the ground,
stealing bits of sunlight
& secret colors from the earth
before giving water's clarity
to our noble, straw mats.

& yet, her hands are nothing like the rain
as she weaves together grasses
with the slowness of fog,
until the whole house flourishes like a forest
woven out of humble wood.

Wise are those comforting hands
that drive off winter
with wide cozy blankets,
& hide us from the cold.

This is how I knew her:
bent over warp & weft,
as if lighting a fire
or setting a table—
her tireless hands
weaving vigils
with stars & wind.

A River Makes Its Way Through the City

Translated by Miller Williams

A river makes its way through the city.
The houses pass slowly.
The sky also passes, immobile
that sometimes was enraptured by the birds.

The river brings the language of the snow.
It is the River of Coal, out of season a stream.

Left behind are bridges
made of immemorial wood
tasted by the river.

Its rhythm still holds the echoes of children
playing in the sand.

Nobody knows if this winter will be the same.

The river cuts into the city
like a shadow moving to the suburbs,
divides it whimsically
before falling into the sea.

Over an old bridge
pass cars and carts loaded down with wood
making the plain heart of the wood
shake.

The Country House

Translated by July Westhale

The damp takes over the yard,
without mills or ditches to draw water from.
This has always been lonely land.
No sunflowers or exuberant vegetables
stretch to greet the sky,
and this is fine. Gray wooden fences
stand deformed by wind, and a tender moss
that either never knew—or forgot—the sun.

The house has the attitude
of countless winters, the language of downpours
destroying rooftops. The rain
is the belltower where no pigeons live,
ringing in legends all afternoon,
no thoughts at all to the domestic.
My grandfather grew old with this land.
He was a watchman of orchards
and crops, up before the dew
with his shovel and his cigar,
warming the earth with his conversation,
protecting it from grand frosts.

The yard behind the house is wrinkled
and hard, without fruit trees
or irrigation. But the roots protect
their secret mansions in all seasons,
like fertilized tenderness,
like beloved underground light.

The Eternity of Corners

Translated by July Westhale

The old corners of the house are
prisoners of moss and time.

Each one has its distinct face,
full of shadow, or full of the sun's
absence, no room for surprise at Spring's delay.

They are taciturn echos of their former
moments, impossible to recover now.
Smiles between bodies, fruit
placed in palms. Silent
and eternal, like an ancient map,
or a recurring dream, from a time
when an endless expedition
seemed easier than waiting for rain.

In this house there were books—
whose heroes we aspired to be—
that fell from our knees
when the notes of an organ
disturbed the streets. There was
my father's poncho, waiting
for his hand and his horse.
The memory shakes
from its roots, awakening the hidden:
a fear of winter, a moment
in the courtyard threatened by hail,
a girl is calling to the birds by name.

Anyone who comes looking for forgotten
secrets—and reaches them—is reborn again.

The Visit

Translated by Felipe Acevedo Riquelme

I have not dared to awaken the secret of time
thus I have come quietly,
like a slow leaf beneath water,
to this place where everyone sleeps and dreams.

Barely could the stillness of pines be noticed,
barely was the space broken by pigeons left behind.
The day was the peace rising from the ground.

I walked as in an abandoned city
autumn had the same color as the fog,
when going through its narrow pathways
listening to my own footsteps as if they came from afar
was just like a child's fear of darkness.

I would touch the fountains stained by violent rust,
I would simply lift a leaf or a twig,
I would feel around the silent dwellings,
I would feel around the air as if I were a blind man,
for it was so long since I had been there
awed by things I had never believed in before,
and I was not feeling the southern wind cooling my face,
nor the possibility that the sky might suddenly change,
because never had I felt more alone
than when gazing at this plot of land
with flowers looking for a sun that did not exist,
as if everything was made for something uncanny,
looking at myself from within and yearning to know.

Perhaps that is why there are bells
that toll to be heard by no one,
bells made out of haze flying in the rain,
and I would feel growing the grass and crawling the worms,
I would feel the dampness as if it were a wall,
and words were my sole possession.
I talked to them about all these years.
I asked them about certain things,
knowing I would never receive an answer,
because no one would be able to utter them
and because I was only just passing by.

The Ghosts

Translated by Mathew Weitman

for Jorge Teillier

They arrive suddenly
in a rain-filled afternoon—
as the gravedigger rises from the Northwest
in the ancient cemetery—
& drift across the bay & slanted streets
where the leaves no longer reign.

It grows dark & cold,
until the silhouettes
of the old coal-pontoons finally disappear.

& it will be childhood again:
sleepless in a shadowed room, faintly breathing.
& the whole house will be filled with them—
they will surround even the rain & wind
whistling through the wires.

That is how those days passed
in the dampness of a haunted house,
with a grandmother
tender as the word itself.

Back then, it was easy to be astonished—
words were filled with the innumerable secrets
of the ghost towns they passed through,
where Death had driven away even the birds.

Now, the voices that once made them
move & breathe become shadows
on nights when the moon & sea are stilled
to resurrect the old Chilote legends
of illuminated ships with strangely deformed crews.

This is how it will happen.

It is enough to know the gravedigger
will always rise from the Northwest,
with those whose memories are lost beneath the ground,
& touch me with an icy hand.

Return

Translated by Mathew Weitman

One day, we will return to the lost city
—like seasons to a year
or shadows to the afternoon—
& ask about our ancestors
& the river, whose waters
broke the sky.

It will be winter:
in the revival of profound coldness
we will see again
the black smoke of ships cutting the air,
& listen to the small noise of snow
falling through the night.

We will sit at the table like nothing
happened & eat the bread of other days.
A bird crossing the windowsill
will remind us of the pine
forests, where the wind
furiously spins.

We will ask about our ancient friends
while thinking, perhaps,
of another girl's face.
The bar
where old workers gathered
still exists—
they'll invite us over there to drink
& talk of unspoken subjects
no one could forget.

Time is nothing more than a return to other times:
we'll all meet underground someday.
Someone will recognize us
around the corner—
& we'll say hello
from another era.

Real Aural Vividness: On Translating *In the Winter of the Province*

Julia Guez

IT HAS BEEN TWENTY YEARS since I have visited the place where Rolando Cárdenas was born (Punta Arenas) or the city where, fifteen years before I arrived, he died (Santiago). In the poems that make up *En el invierno de la provincia*, the city is abstract, more often than not, unnamed; it isn't described, really; it isn't alive the way Patagonia is absolutely teeming. The small town of Punta Arenas, not far from Torres Del Paine National Park, and the capital city of Santiago are set up as poles. Patagonia is never abstracted, though. Even when Cárdenas seems to be spinning something of a mythology around the geography and geology, the flora and the fauna there; even when he's working through centuries of indigenous, colonial, and post-colonial history rooted in the Southern Cone, Cárdenas renders the scale of this time and place in extraordinary detail. There's something of an ecopoetic *ars poetica* in the poem, "Message For Magallanes (From the Stone)," when he says, "and for people who've only known sun, / I give them your geography, piece by piece." These "pedazos" or "pieces" are sensory details; feelings—states projected upon (or derived from) the landscape; they are images.

In this poem, and so many others, Cárdenas presents these images through simile (a comparison between two things using the word "como"—in English, "like" or "as"). In my translation, many of these similes are rendered as metaphors. In a literal translation, the similes "con tu silencio completo *como* un círculo / creciendo *como* un riguroso y lento musgo" would be set up with the word, "like," as in "your silence . . . like a circle." In my translation, however, these lines are asked to read as metaphors, as in, "your complete silence, a circle / growing like moss, that rigorous, that slow." Instead of using "like" and "like" in this sequence, I reproduce the repetition of "como" with a double-touch on the word, "that." This, to me, protects some of the music in the line and its many long "o" sounds—*silencio, completo, como, circulo, creciendo, como, riguroso, lento, musgo*. In my translation, though, you'll notice repetition of the "c" and "s" sounds with complete, silence, circle, moss, rigorous and slow. The sonic effects are different, of course; they're analogous, though not exactly equivalent. The compression of the simile into a metaphor (requiring the subtraction of the word, "like" or "as," also means to protect the image from any dilution into English (which tends to need many more words to get even the simplest and the most beautiful moments across from the Spanish).

Cárdenas leans, heavily, on sight when producing some of his strongest images. These painterly, often somewhat Romantic images of Patagonia retain the magic of seeing these landscapes through a child's eye. The poems create real vividness aurally, as well: the silence of this land is evoked more often than anything else. Cádenas also lingers on the sound of birdsong, the sound of snow, the sound of the sea "howl[ing]," "the sound of a sheepdog," the sound of the rain, the sound of thunder, and the "lugubrious" sound of the wind. The olfactory makes only a few appearances in this collection. In "Message to Magellanes (From the Stone)," however, there's a reference to:

> the hard wood of your forests,
> the fiber, the fragrance
> lingering in your big heart whose lonelinesses
> ships and cities come from.

The feeling-state most associated with this landscape is loneliness; a sense of "loss" pervades the poems, if not the actual place. Cárdenas grew up where so many of these poems are set. In his childhood, he lost his father first; then, only four years later, he lost his mother. He was only eleven at the time. I can't help reading some of these poems with that part of his experience in mind. Returning for a moment to the fragrance of the wood from Magallanes, I want to highlight the verb at the heart of that image (which I note because I haven't been able to come up with a literal translation that doesn't sound awkward). Ships and cities aren't simply "built" out of the the timber; they don't simply "come" from these forests either (as my own translation suggests). In Cárdenas's phrasing:

> Algo tiene que ver contigo
> el rudo maderamen de tus bosques,
> la fragancia de fibra
> que se queda en tu ancho corazón de soledades
> de donde *van naciendo* navíos y ciudades.

"Naciendo" is the present progressive form of "nacer" which means, literally, to be born. Ships and cities then are born—a literal rendering might suggest they "go on getting born" out of the loneliness, at the very core of this wood. A subtle evocation of a mothering energy, and also a separating, even an orphaning energy associated with both loneliness and the landscape are core to this line, poem, and collection.

Even if you don't know Spanish, you can savor the play of sound in these lines: the assonance of "contigo" and "rudo," the consonance between "fragrancia" and "fibra" and of course, the half-rhyme between "soledades" and "ciudades." As we get caught up in the sound-play, it may be easy to miss the verb in the last line of this sequence. Here and elsewhere, it's important to attend to moments that subtly evoke birth, beginnings, creation, movement, and care on the one hand, and death, endings, destruction, motionlessness, and abandonment or loss on the other. Like the pole set up between Punta Arenas and Santiago—and a pole between the past and present—this mothering and orphaning pole is central to the image system in and beyond *En el invierno de la provincia.*

There are many subtleties in these deceptively simple but deep-feeling poems. Time and space get conflated; present and past merge, too; the geological forms that make Patagonia so astonishing meet high-lyrical forms no less astonishing, in their own way. These translations mean to bring as much of this astonishment over as they can.

Someone Will Recognize Us Around This Corner

Ramón Díaz Eterovic

Translated by Daniela Anaís Jara Guevara and Valentina Merino Amigo. Berlin, Germany, 17 October 2024.

MY FIRST ENCOUNTER WITH THE POET Rolando Cárdenas was through one of his books. I was in secondary school and in one of the bookshelves of the library of the Liceo de Hombres de Punta Arenas,[18] I discovered a copy of the book *En el invierno de la provincia*. Until then, I had only heard of him a few times. I knew, for example, that he was a Magellanic poet, and who in those years—at the beginning of the 70's—began to receive his first acclaim from reviewers and journalists. That Jorge Teillier had defined his work as "poetry of the hearth."

I read the book with novel enthusiasm. My world was portrayed in his poems, the streets of Punta Arenas, its weather, its landscape, the snow, and the men who lived there. It was like seeing myself in a mirror. At the same time, I felt that I could not

[18] See footnote 1

be the same person after reading those lines. I was transformed. What's more, Rolando Cárdenas's poetry deviated from the style of other Magellanic poets. Though he used many images, his scenery contained something more profound than mere description: an understanding of the human condition through a telluric and metaphysical gaze. Being from the same place, it was not hard for me to feel attracted to his poetry and vision of the world. His verses reproduced our village, and each one of its images belonged to me, these precious treasures.

Years later, I had my own personal encounter with Rolando Cárdenas. It was in 1980, during a poetry cycle at the Taller de Arte Contemporáneo, a cultural center led by two other Magellanic men who knew Cárdenas's poetry well: Luis Aravena Azócar and Patricio Lanfranco. When it was his turn to read, he read his poems with grand, ceremonial gestures when he wanted to denote the transcendental. His pauses grew large in the spaces between the bodies of those listening; the Austral geography and his ancestors' names came back to life under the spell of words. He was a poet who unveiled his secrets slowly, and the rhythm of his images followed. Although that night we did not talk much—maybe because we both were characterized by the cultural silence of the Magellanic people—a friendship with one of my most beloved poets was born that night.

A few days later, we ran into each other at the bar La Unión Chica, a place he would often meet other writers. This bar was legendary, located at Nueva York Street—a few blocks away from the Civic District of Santiago—with ancient wooden tables and the sound of dice being scattered, where Jorge Teillier, Eduardo Molina Ventura, Carlos Olivarez, Álvaro Ruiz, Roberto Araya Gallegos, Enrique Valdés, Iván Teillier, Juan Guzmán Paredes, Aristóteles España, Ramón Carmona, and the artist Germán Arestizábal used to spend time. Sometimes, Gonzalo Rojas, Nicanor Parra, Gonzalo Drago, Mario Ferrero, and Francisco Coloane showed up as well, among many others that would make that bar a meeting spot, of poetic oasis, while beyond the swinging of its door, life was painted with the black tone of the dictatorship. Cárdenas says in one of his poems: "It is nice to sit among friends and glasses, to see how everyone leaves something of their own in the music that drives and transforms them into beings without bones, while the night climbs over the walls . . . " That bar was a mandatory meeting spot for many writers and poets and even, at some time, a sort of navigation log was kept in there where each person recorded their ideas or references for attendance: a book that would go around from hand to hand. Perhaps something Teillier still owns. In the bar La Unión Chica, there was always someone ready to talk about literature or raise a friendly glass. As the poet Marino Muñoz Lagos recalls, "leaning on his elbows on the counter, Rolando Cárdenas peered through the fog of cigarette smoke and saw that far away south, whose tenacious blizzards and transparent frost seemed always to call him."

The afternoon of our first encounter, Rolando Cárdenas was standing next to the bar, buttoned into his woolen jacket, well-groomed, with silver hair and an energizing, sudden smile that reached his eyes. His face—not so good-looking due to his busted nose, like a beaten-up boxer—had the usual seriousness, and in the distance, he looked like a small old man, half asleep among the noise of the regulars. He was wearing his customary tie and, in his reach was an envelope with old newspapers and letters. After many glasses of wine, Rolando Cárdenas gifted me his book *Poemas Migratorios* for which he had received the Pedro de Oña award of the Ñuñoa City Hall. We talked about the poetry of our province.

That encounter birthed a great affection. Rolando Cárdenas had an inner strength that mismatched what many thought when meeting him for the first time. He was a poet who was proud of his job of being a poet, who knew the different schools of Chilean poetry—as few do—and who used to talk about poetry with a deep understanding of the respect it deserves. His most frequent advice was to come close to poetry with seriousness, without rush, sheltered by the knowledge of the work of other poets, to know that being a poet is more related to silence than to loudness. He was also proud; he was a man who knew his worth. His solitude was a thought-out gesture. He retreated to it when existence itself stopped bringing the joy and colors that he liked, when many of his friends had to leave the country, and, most of all, when poetry—what he loved the most—turned into the job of the dead, nearer to fear than to anything else.

Rolando's reserved and serious character was not devoid of a sense of humor. He knew how to laugh. But whenever necessary, as if all the strength of his ancestors were part of him. Like few others, Cárdenas was a generous soul, always open to friendship or mentorship. He showed great interest in his friends' work, rejoicing at every new publication, and always ready to provide an opinion, often of certainty. One example was his sheer enthusiasm when the poetry magazine *La gota pura* was born out of the bar La Unión Chica. Dozens of pages represented those of us who gathered there and many other writers living in the provinces, or far away from Chile.

Rolando Cárdenas was a simple man. He was a friend to silence. His small frame—a motive for constant teasing—held a big heart, open to the worries of others. Perhaps it is because of where he was from that he acquired a taciturn attitude: introverted, reflexive, given to meditation and nostalgia, suspicious of timidity, carrying the mistrust of the Austral man who had not yet gotten used to the hustle and bustle of the capital.

Despite our age difference, we shared much in common. We spoke at length of our collective provincial experiences: the same streets, the memory of a certain food, the place we carried with us where we went.

I feel again that his passing was premature and unfair. His poetry should have had the recognition that it was denied, because we well know that in the tiny world of our literature, appearance matters more than the truth. An empty scream is more important than the fecund silence, to which Rolando Cárdenas was so faithful.

I remember Rolando sharing with other poets, singing folkloric songs in the middle of the night. Sometimes plucking a guitar. I remember his handwriting on the wall of Refugio López Velarde: "Why should you care what I care."[19] Today, almost coinciding with his death, you can no longer see the writing.

I remember Rolando Cárdenas walking through the snowy streets of Punta Arenas, oddly cheerful, feeling "the little noises of the snow" under his feet, showing me places he spent his adolescence.

I never saw him happier. I quoted a line of his back to him: "Someone will recognize us around the corner. It will be like a greeting from another age." He smiled, and responded that he was not a stranger, the places we passed were his memories. They lived for him alongside his ancestors and his childhood, and they were always with him.

---

[19] It is a word play that is grammatically incorrect. Original: "Que te importa a mí."

Rolando Cárdenas playing drums (above) and guitar (right facing page).

Scan the QR code to hear Cardenas's poem "From Now On I Love You," sung by Jorge Aravena Llanca.

Characters of My City, 1964

Translated by July Westhale

The Organ Grinder

I remember the organ grinder. Everyone does. I remember him as if he were outside my own house, my own street in the snowy province. Like an overly obsessive musical note. Like returning to childhood that is much too far away, contemplating the innately familiar as through the window, an old melody running through it all like a breeze of good fortune.

Like rescuing a kite trapped in a live wire.

The ancient melody disappears now, in the muddy next street over, with the organ grinder and his drum man. The ragged, boisterous children follow them.

There it is again, in the distance. A return to childhood. Rescuing the kite. Emerging from the earth.

The Chicken Thief

He is a late night character, an expert climber, both born from and confused by shadow. A certain dark hour is his most willing companion, always willing to open doors or fences. It is silent work. His hands are agile and his face, impenetrable. His eyes are accustomed to piercing obscurity for prey.

Chicken thief, I remember, on mouths scattered through all towns. A wake of plundered coops.

Avid scoundrel in his usual task. There he goes with his sack, to barter for bread or wine or to calm his chronic hunger, slipping like a specter, away from the light.

The Birdkeeper

What a hubbub of colors and languages the birdkeeper drags about. His voice has learned hidden care and tones to better converse with his flocks.

Perhaps because he has taken the sky from them, he moves with a slight incline in his weary step. Perhaps because of the constant rumbling of wings, he cannot dream of flying. He walks with his own words buried slightly inside him.

A dull uproar: the colored trills of the birds and the thoughts of the birdkeeper sway slowly in the air as a beautiful, feathered form advances.

From on high, up there: an insistent invitation to blue, to the immense everything, where they are inhabitants of a winged kingdom.

The Flag Seller

The city square, and the sun in it. A cordial invitation to banish Sunday morning's laziness. To join the celebration of the people with their wafers and balloons. A joy of color as the flag seller slips through the crowds. All of them on a single pole, in a tight bundle, like a sustained embrace.

This man from our town knows to keep his hands soft when making a kite. Through them flows the narrow geography, and the forces of changing elements that govern us.

A secret craftsman with an enthusiastic trade. A small wonder, three pieces of colored paper and its single star, guardian of the winter sun.

The Florist

With a flower in his ear and a chorus jumping in his mouth, the most auspicious season has arrived in a large wicker basket.

He strides to every garden with a vigorous arm, to every orchard, the earth itself. The arm gathers all colors and aromas into humid, cheerful merchandise. He will dress the mantle of the family party as a party itself, next to the bread, where faces and hands meet.

In the distance, the stentorian cry of the florist breaks the morning street in two, leaving in its wake the auspicious season's message, floating lightly in the air.

Characters from my City *was originally published in collaboration with the artist Guillermo Deisler (Ediciones Mimbre, 1964). Printed on kite paper, the book included original prints made by Deisler alongside each poem. Above: Deisler's engraving plate from "The Florist."*

The Papeleros[20]

They are born from the morning mist. Unable to emerge except with winter himself, incorporated into him as if part of a sick center.

Bent over the saw, bent over countless jars as if searching for their own faces, they disappear at the end of each day as if devoured by anguish.

I have seen them, indifferent to the street as it awakens, rummaging through remains, locating the crystallized daily bread, a warm and sorry bed of refuse, the indispensable wine.

Nomadic men in doorways, disheveled and pallid with their smokey hair, enormous bags of grief on their backs, born into a life of regret, colorless and cold, like their everyday, ruined dreams.

[20] Translator's note: this word, whose approximation in English seems to be "paper sorters," was much debated and agonized over. In the end, considering the class context and the word's current obscurity /passing out of colloquial fashion, I kept the original Spanish to preserve the distance the word denotes.

The Knife Sharpener

The sparks rise from the grindstone, like tiny shooting stars, scratching the air with their impermanence. The man working, inclined over his knife. A long, dry noise and the rhythmic sounds of the wheel surround him like a fog. He is a necessary presence, a meager figure in working class neighborhoods.

He will call on every house.

Everything is light in his hands: the sparks, and the frosted iron with its metallic reflection. The wheel never stops, and its sound travels everywhere. The tool will flash, renewed with the elemental purpose of cutting food, and the knife sharpener will be gone, lost in the twists and turns of other streets, knocking on other doors.

Migratory Poems, 1974

Translated by Mary Ann Christensen

The Earth Travels and Is Encircled by the Sea

The earth travels and is encircled by the sea,
this earth so scattered in such mysterious sea.
If she changes places, her voracity follows us without rest,
if we move away from him, he keeps resounding within us.

We have not chosen this earth,
she has dwelled in us since with her nocturnal light,
with that clarity that precedes the rain,
with the snow that whitens in the nights of gnarled trees,
with her deepest darkness in her sleeping greenery,
and with all the brusqueness at the onset of her catastrophes.
To grow accustomed to her, we invoke the sun.

We have not sought this immemorial water,
this water that floods and devours us relentlessly,
though we have lived surrounded by its brackish dampness;
for from its reeling center the green ocean is born,
that holds all things in its undertow,
from his vastness the horizon
from his outstretched form comes its harmonious surge.

One cannot recognize
all beings now parted by the waters;
you cannot rebuild all the lives
in those houses that also drift away,
beings and houses which, in the mist of distance,
leave us only with faces dissolving
like one mirror in front of another, to infinity,
in these lands that separate in silence.

The earth travels and is encircled by the sea,
this winged encasing that slowly drifts
with all our absent ones that we carry within,
with the names of things in a blank memory,
with its ghosts of time emerging from the ice
and winter unchanging like a lone horse on the plain,
its winds rebuilding the ancient fear,
with its compressed solitude transmitted by blood
from which we have arisen, like from the depths of a great
    summertide,
to bear witness to something we only sense,
to that which brushes us with its breath under an untouched sky,
in this drift, surrounded by water.

The Tamer

Man and horse were made for each other
from the very beginning, to measure their strength.
But man carried a distant secret,
that was also his maritime pride:
dexterity and wisdom mastered the other,
the other wild one, tempestuous and unbridled across horizons.

And meant to be at sea or horseback,
he, with feet on solid ground, was slow and taciturn,
with the attitude of a tenuous tree,
or of a man who does not know his home;
so remote and enigmatic,
as if the river of his blood had stopped flowing.

It had to be on a young stallion
where he would recover his powerful bearing,
the distant lineage of tamers, of other plains
bequeathed by an ancestor.

Man and horse
will become an unhearing struggle bound in wrath,
a wild embrace that turns and falls into the solitude
facing the fierce lash of the western wind,
splintering the mirror of that boundless space
with a panting, primitive murmur,
with a roar that will not be contained and devours the hills,
making the plains and their hidden rivers tremble,
hounded by the ferocity and violence of those untamed lands.

What will remain is exactly
a cloud of dust and *coirón* blades drifting away,
and a thick, misshapen scent
of sweat and fatigue.

It was the root that transfigured him,
the heaviest of secrets, ready to spill—
his natural knowledge for sensing the rain,
his mantle prepared for every cold southern wind,
the one with the weathered face and the decisive silence.
Now he lies struck down by an ancient horse.

Roofing Ceremony

At dawn they left behind the last streets of the city
and ventured into the nearby hills,
sure and confident,
as if searching for the sea
that echoed beyond those ridges.

They were all coastal dwellers.
They had left their small islands and villages
for this north wind
that tosses on them in long, cutting gusts,
for this hard frost and this violent land
and I have never asked them why.

That is why they laughed when they caught the ancient, salty scent
of the sea
that pursued them with its unbridled fierceness,
their years without memory and its wisdom.

Sometimes they remembered how a seafarer once cursed it,
yet here they had come, and couldn't keep still.
Stopped in the middle of the night,
their words crossed slowly through time:
In this place they would firmly defy the wind and the rain,
lifted by my hands, from which all things were born.

While they gathered around bread and wine
resting from the day's labor,
they told me that everything the eye could reach
was the fruit of long and wearisome years of labor.

"They are your ancestors," they said,
"and of those who now settle these hills,
who with their blood help raise these foundations."

Someone looked to the sky to predict the fair weather,
glanced at the calm spirals of smoke
from neighboring homes,
took up his hammer, and whistling an old tune,
walked away through the freshly raised beams
to be with them until sundown.

White Nights

And it was a light that seemed to be there at every hour,
when the days began to lengthen,
bending toward slow, snow-covered lands.

It beamed without boundaries
in an almost silent chore,
from red skies thick with hills,
where birds sailed late into the evening.
It also seemed to come by sea,
with a mysterious murmur and an ashen hue.

Ancient clarity of the ice lingering there
since the first polar night,
enacting a remote rite that stilled the shadows
and yet, at once, lapsed on.

It stayed with us for long hours,
as if it could take sleep or weariness from us,
growing old with the grasslands and the wind.

Like a memory that floods everything,
those southern days emerge
from the time of man who lost his shadow,
because those nights, faintly lit,
come from the ice, the sea, and the red sky
and seemed not at all strange in that scattered land,
circling that house
lost in a great white breath.

The Silences

Sometimes in the house
the only sound was the crackling of wood in the stove
and the rhythmic hum of the spinning winder
where grandmother lost herself.

All gathered, all silent,
as if called to solemnly preside over winter,
with a posture much like that in night dreams
but with two lives behind those years:
one, with thousands of blanched trees,
and the other, allowing the silence of now to grow
with the gale circling this house.

The crackling wood devours their words,
and the turns of the winder withdraw and lull them.

On the inside, the house is a wooden silence,
but after so much time,
someone stirs from their seat and moves toward the fire,
for some stray raindrop that bubbled in the tub
is reason enough to comment briefly on the cloudless sky.

Warp

It was the vine-like hand of the house
that tenderly took the white ball of yarn
and made it roll along the wood.
The entire room slowly covered itself
with a broad layer the color of crystalline water,
and the entire house became an island,
softly carried by the wind
and the current of the highest tide
amid a vast whitened silence.

It was the same snow brought by that hand that now will
    not touch me,
a hand that never tired
of choosing the seeds for planting,
of searching for forgotten toys,
of picking timber in a foggy forest one morning
and transforming it into sweet, polished tools.

Something was changing before my eyes,
resembling no secrets,
like being still beneath a dizzying sky and traveling with it,
or facing a meadow with a figure crouched before me.

My arm was the one that tired or wandered
in this task of playing on bended knees,
but from the other side of the meadow
emerged that which called me by my name.

I had not finished leaning forward in a gesture of awe
before the disappearing ball of yarn,

the weave advancing to reach the other shore
when suddenly the silence of the house deepened,
as if winter's enemy,
weary of searching for me in its midst,
had decided to undo the entire warp,
to turn its worn eyes
toward the light of its village from where it came to know me.

The Summer Winds

They say goodbye from every corner,
then rush back fleeing the sky,
tangling useless ropes in the rigging
of old sailing ships that never launch.

This business of the wind
is a matter no one discusses much anymore
when gathered at the table are bread and friendship.

If we listen in silence
we'll hear it pulling away,
as if hiding forever among ruins,
only to return like those ghosts of time,
shaking doors and shutters
we forgot to close,
scaring the birds in the courtyard,
or playing with hats as if they were birds.

Once, we wrote a simple homage
on the dust that it carried from the hills—
a name, one that never grows old.

Once, sad winds
were the rough hands of my father
preparing bitter *mate*,
or strumming an old rustic guitar,
the day dying between whistles of wind
and leafless, rainless trees
to multiply the moon in the window.

One Day Kren[21] Did Not Keep His Flames

There's no other way to recognise the facts
than to remove oneself, far,
—like from my home—
perhaps barely guessing,
or clutching almost in despair
to that unsettling, devilish way
of stopping the afternoon.

Just like this, you stopped before me,
fiercely brown-skinned
with your tenderness and your words full of cold
despite the sun
that did not keep its flames.

[21] Kren: a word of Selk-nam origin meaning "sun."

Encounter

The city lay still,
waiting for the fall of afternoon
with its great red clouds behind those hills
that change color at a distance depending on the weather.

I was returning to speak
with those who still lived and awaited me.
From so far, I always received news
of everything and everyone, but it was not the same
as being there, perfectly unknown,
looking toward all the streets and corners,
free to walk anywhere
by just wishing for it.

At every step I found something that made me change,
though things remained there, immutable,
as if ready to carry me back
to the clear, remote mornings of the most distant childhood.

Also, the constant presence of the sea
greeted me, stirring along the Strait.
It appeared suddenly, distant to my senses,
as if rising from the very silence of the street
and the joy of my old discoveries.
After so many years,
it was absurd to meet
and not have time to feel surprise or greet each other,
and for simply nothing to happen.

Edelweiss

Like a shadow of the white light of ice,
growing from the secret of the most dormant water,
the earth's spring makes you more distant,
your blue transparency pushing back, the darkest sea
vigilant of the mighty flight of eagles—
a brief, impalpable statue
shaken by the summit's winds,
the winds from the peak of the most dizzying nights.

Silent in your form,
you shine by day,
a pure, invisible tear made of frost's crystal,
ready to flee the troubled earthbound
to where no one dwells more untouched in your midday height,
in the shrunken air of your seeming center,
far from the warm air that circles the hills,
a precise flower of winter from which you know how to bud,
extraterrestrial daughter of a white memory;
because once
the men of the valleys heard from you,
and then you peeped to the quarters of their deepest eyes.

From no root,
from no branch do you detach,
yet suddenly you flash
like the re-emergence of a star—
from no transit,
from no shore of time,
but from the memory of those who believe in your wait on the
summits,

from those who predict you in the mirror of the sky,
of your unknown home that turns with the earth,
and with the breath that tries to cloud your limpid cup,
with the face searching its image in the place of your calling
at the foot of the wall, toward high migrations
finding the trembling hand that touches a dream.

Absent in the Rooms

Toward the center of the most dormant earth,
that space invariably invoked,
a foreign guest where I one time dwelled
when those we once loved no longer breathe beside us
and return to their cold darkness,
worn and without grasp,
absent even from their own departure,
unknowns wandering the summer twilights
with countless questions,
unaware they themselves hold the answer.

There lies a mirror that will no longer reflect their faces,
the spring that appears they cannot understand,
the resonance of the sea at the foot of the city,
the sky descending softly with snow of another time
upon their cracked materials, far from all light.
Evoked silently in empty rooms,
they rise from my substance, solitary, moving in the opposite
direction,
like watching my slow blood gathered,
the immemorial rain that does not hate the earth
as it does the one who strips it from the tree,
the tree from its nests,
the nests from its birds,
the birds from their vital space
and to this boundless shore,
the disposition to return, recentered, to my ancient origin.

Without those who then kept us in faith,
the disappeared, scorched in their own fire,

will not recognise my face among other beings.
Deprived of those who once held a place beside me,
vegetatively vast,
so absorbed as if I reconstruct for the last time
those who crossed these thresholds repeatedly.
I would not know them in their new earthly labors,
for they did not look within the clear fountain,
nor knew how to love us except in a manner forced,
dizzyingly pale when reaching their deaths,
situated so far away that it truly does not amaze me,
as if they had never been inside me,
as if I had never moved from my place,
as if the immense night turned with the earth around my center.

The Invoked Fruit

It is a dark fruit I now invoke,
a small circle rescued from the night
by its spell, we return from anywhere
towards that same point we one day left behind
forgotten the eyes where we left something of ourselves,
to reunite with that unwavering space that truly belongs to us.

Someone feeds bittersweetly on your body,
someone who is not alone on the damp hills,
but with all those who have tasted you,
the first who left behind other names, other suns,
those who remained by your side through the most violent of winds,
the most violent wind that cannot knock you over,
that pushes and leaves houses adrift,
and bends passersby, exhausted from fighting it,
because at the beginning, the past is a flight
that only returning can cease,
someone who hearkens within, devouring themselves,
and calls forth your brief substance
from the shadow of their bleakest being.

It is a return to find all faces,
a life elapsed that we encompass in a single glance,
a lamp we harbor in a pure gesture,
for the new discovery in the region of great silence,
of the memory that knocks at a sleeping door,
or of the blood fulfilling the urgent desire of its course,
to find you with that light that never ends
or dies out with a single breath
in those scattered lands that were once reunited,

completing the rite that darkens the mouth
beneath a vigilant sky.

It is a dark fruit we will invoke one day,
the fruit of winter at the earth's shore.
glistening in the deep memory
with its berry-like shape of *calafate*
for the awaited return,
as sweet an act as any.

The Ghost of the Evangelistas Lighthouse

Far from the signals of the coast,
held in the most distant depths of the planet,
like four shadows emerging from the sea.
Only time beyond the archipelagos,
time turned into a desperately blank horizon,
a stubborn wind clinging with a roar
to thick, shattered water, tirelessly.

Nothing interrupted that solitude that had no beginning or end,
not even the passage from day to night.
But then the ravine must have trembled when those great
 continents,
wandering beneath the sea, emerged—perhaps like giant
 wounded whales
swaying slowly and strangely
from marine cataclysms a millennia old.
And spinning endlessly in the middle of the ocean—

master of the source it won't reveal
because only the sea keeps its secrets forever—
they remain unusually eternal,
lost in the fog, more distant and somber,
as if returning to their ancient solitude,
the solitude of stone and water.

And it was a rigorous water penetrating the rock
like silence in a large house,
carving hollows in its eternal undertow,
with salt encrusting its small material,
enclosing in a white ring that inaccessible world

in a precise process,
pushed toward the last shores
by the desolate wind of the Strait,
with only moss and lichens growing in its folds,
under the weight of other constellations.
That petrified, harsh wet air was broken
by brief flutters in solitary circles
of the misty, blackish flight of "La Remolinera"
like a miniscule sign of lasting and frozen life.
Everything else was distant and dark on the four crags.

Death here was a violent omen,
an essential substance breathing in shadows,
twisting the good course of vessels,
driving them away from the white breath of the lighthouse
that uprightly challenged the black height
between barriered, gray, granite walls,
necessarily presented there to pierce the night,
guiding errant ships
through labyrinths of notches, channels, and reefs
that appear and disappear amid squalls and ocean waves.
Death in the storm, silent and cold
between the abyss of the sea and the sky.

Here was a certainty, terrible and true
that stabbed like a delirious bite between two lighthouse
    keepers,
prisoners of unending months of solitude
and of unleashed, ruthless elements
that relentlessly marked them with their icy breath.
And like a merciless origin of madness,
with no chance to live without her then,
a great lonely soul felt silence grow like a chill,

watching earthly traffic halt little by little,
the word and fatigue of the indispensable companion,
unable to stop the call of that hidden force
claiming her own with each minute amid gusts of wind and water,
fearsome and imperative in her demands,
slowly biting the lacerated flesh,
wanting to hold him forever in her steel-gray crags,
leaving him the maddened inhabitant of his high tower,
absolute master of that beacon of safe passage,
only a hallucinated, freezing automaton
sweetly wrapping his body in tar.

Sleepy was he who descended to wander the sea,
defeated by that heavy and powerful lethargy,
and no one will ever rouse his fixed eyes,
and he will have no respite wandering over flat landscapes,
immaterial and restless over the rocks,
just a tiny cry that swirls and falls and is never heard,
returns and is lost among slippery walls of algae and mists,
absorbed and intangible in its liquid world,
rolling through intangible rain and taciturn,
his steps tumbling down concavities,
abandoned like the last being of a destroyed planet,
stubbornly alone on his unremitting journey,
spilled and transparent as if sprung from light or ice,
cold as the strained air before his life
dragged downward,
toward a time without past or without measure
his tarred death,
his imponderable shadow.

Hills That Have Ceased to Be

In the ocean of those nights
I paused with my signs, scattering
away from those hills that have ceased to be,
(today they must be dotted with red rooftops),
from the snow on the solitude of Sundays,
and that icy water that has surrounded us always
and from fire that separated us from winter.

A time definitively elapsed and forgotten
by that decision
to hide near this other side of the sea.

Now it was your deep voice,
deep as resonating wood softly touched,
tenaciously distant from what wasn't this secret,
ready to leave behind what had shamed us,
to rebuild everything in this lost house beneath the sky,
an alliance suddenly awakened.

Silence was also a silence full of voices
that came with sleep
brimmed with the hidden sounds of night and earth.

Without a doubt, you were an absent horizon,
white and asleep,
one who doesn't hear me in her briny moisture,
but in a sudden gesture draws me closer,
more than the foam preparing from afar,
distant from your eyes darkened by the afternoon.

You were far more than the cold morning air
that never managed to penetrate that small hiding place near the sea.

Selk'nam[22]

It was in that distant land, at the dawn of bonfires,
where plains were lashed by merciless gales,
sometimes crossed by flocks of cara-cara or black-faced ibis,
beneath a pale sun that seemed from another time.

It's possible it was not always so,
like those countless lagoons
that formed in winter and vanished in summer
between mountain chains that suddenly perish in the Beagle
Channel,
and forests thick with *calafates, maitenes,* and *canelos.*

In that Antarctic thicket,
in that heavy, green-scented air,
laden with the deformed breath of giant trees, rotting
from the start of the Strait to Navarino,
they appeared in the midst of rain,
as if emerged from distant continent of ice,
just as if ripped from the white light time of night
at the origin of the great family.

Nomads of their own remoteness,
they crossed the silences with the old wisdom of their gods,
knowers of the magic of Festuca
that grows south of Río Grande,
and which, before shedding its green blades,
turns into an astounding autumn purple,
eternal owners of their primordial solitude
in their fragile tents, conical like bell towers.

---

[22] The Selk'nam, also known as the Onawo or Ona people, are an indigenous people in the Patagonian region of southern Argentina and Chile, including the Tierra del Fuego islands.

All they needed was oak for their bows,
and the sea for their sustenance,
before the simple task of their deaths
at however many pounds sterling per head,
and still, they could celebrate the arrival of fair weather.

adorning their faces with colors of red earth
or the charred bones of *guanacos*.

Come from the water,
or rather from ice
when the poles began to shift,
today they retreat nestled inside a tree trunk through the
archipelagos,
toward the same solitude of their dreams,
like the deepest sleep
of that ancient and strange land,
blending with the sea mist,
the sky, and the stones,
to merge forever with the stars, the hills, and the fjords,
to petrify in the water.

From This Old House So Foreign to the Others

In every still thing in the night
dwells that immemorial time
that devours me like a strange fruit,
more than an ancient dream lingering in the blood
where faces are hard to distinguish
and in its blurred ring it envelops us,
destroys us, and feeds us.

Unknowingly, we have lived aware of that murmur
from which you emerged, foreign and pensive,
lying beside me like a vast white plain,
returning to my strained, southern origin,
recovering part of that unknown space,
from this old house so foreign to others,
like my inherited features that were also yours as well,
where I am not surprised by your mouth that now calls me,
nor your open hands,
nor your gestures
that neither hide nor distance you.

Words were created for that lamp of the shadows
that revealed your island carved in ancient sandstone.
until it became land violently spilled to the sun.
I learned of the first time you saw the dull of your eyes
blossom, by the highest, loudest waves
in their pilgrimage across the sea,
of the uncertain return of boats at daybreak

gently crossing the Chilote channels,
and above, the sweeping flight of lapwings.

So far behind those walls,
like a memory inside another more fruitful one,
the rainbow and its silent curve
over the island of crimson afternoons,
with that clear play of light and water as the only trace,
the rolling stones over the hills,
homelands where distant kin live unhurried, taciturn,
where the tempests harmonize men.

This impartial land that binds us
has been slowly transforming us:
I have a face unknown to me, forgotten,
you stand with a village scarf before the river,
laughing uproariously and certain beneath the sun,
and I cannot help but think of yours or mine,
with black shawls given tirelessly to their labours,
you are without your childhood,
afraid of the tiny, pink worms of the sowings.
I am, instead,
the one who in every fold of day or night sees your face,
the gathered shadows or all the winters at the heart of that
  transparency,
a dampened heart
in which I will never dwell.

The night does not weigh,
become another ghost among the walls,
someone certain they breathed your closeness
by that distant shore where you fall silent,
almost absent in the stance of the deepest sky,
illuminated snow covering a dark earth.

Absolutes and identical after recognizing each other
at that door no one else can cross,
where you continue in countless silences,
that who returns from their dream
the tenderness of wanting to utter a name
is the only one who can leave in your hands
"this cup of *yatui* flower water for forgetting."

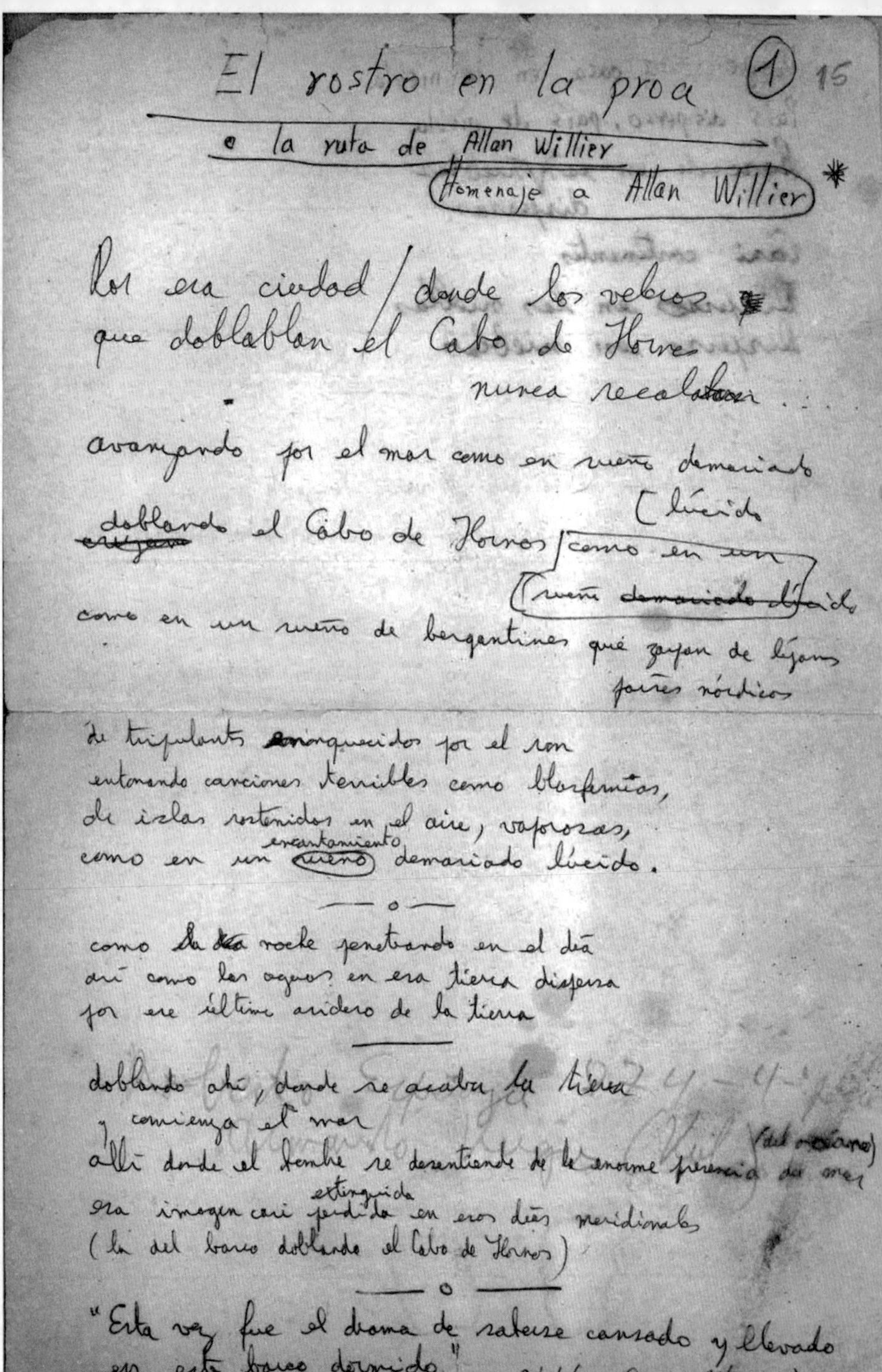
El rostro en la proa (1) 15

o la ruta de Allan Willier

(Homenaje a Allan Willier) *

Por esa ciudad / donde los veleros
que doblaban el Cabo de Hornos
nunca recalaban...

avanzando por el mar como en sueño demasiado [lúcido

~~cruzan~~ doblando el Cabo de Hornos [como en un sueño ~~demasiado lúcido~~]

como en un sueño de bergantines que zarpan de lejanos
países nórdicos

de tripulantes ~~en~~ enronquecidos por el ron
entonando canciones terribles como blasfemias,
de islas sostenidas en el aire, vaporosas,
como en un (~~sueño~~) encantamiento demasiado lúcido.

— o —

como ~~la día~~ noche penetrando en el día
así como las aguas en esa tierra dispersa
por ese último asidero de la tierra

———

doblando ahí, donde se acaba la tierra
y comienza el mar
allí donde el hombre se desentiende de la enorme presencia (del océano) del mar
esa imagen casi ~~perdida~~ extinguida en esos días meridionales
(la del barco doblando el Cabo de Hornos)

— o —

"Esta vez fue el drama de saberse cansado y llevado
en este barco dormido." Adolfo Couve (Nación)

Draft of "The Face on the Bow, or the route of Allan Williers" pg.1

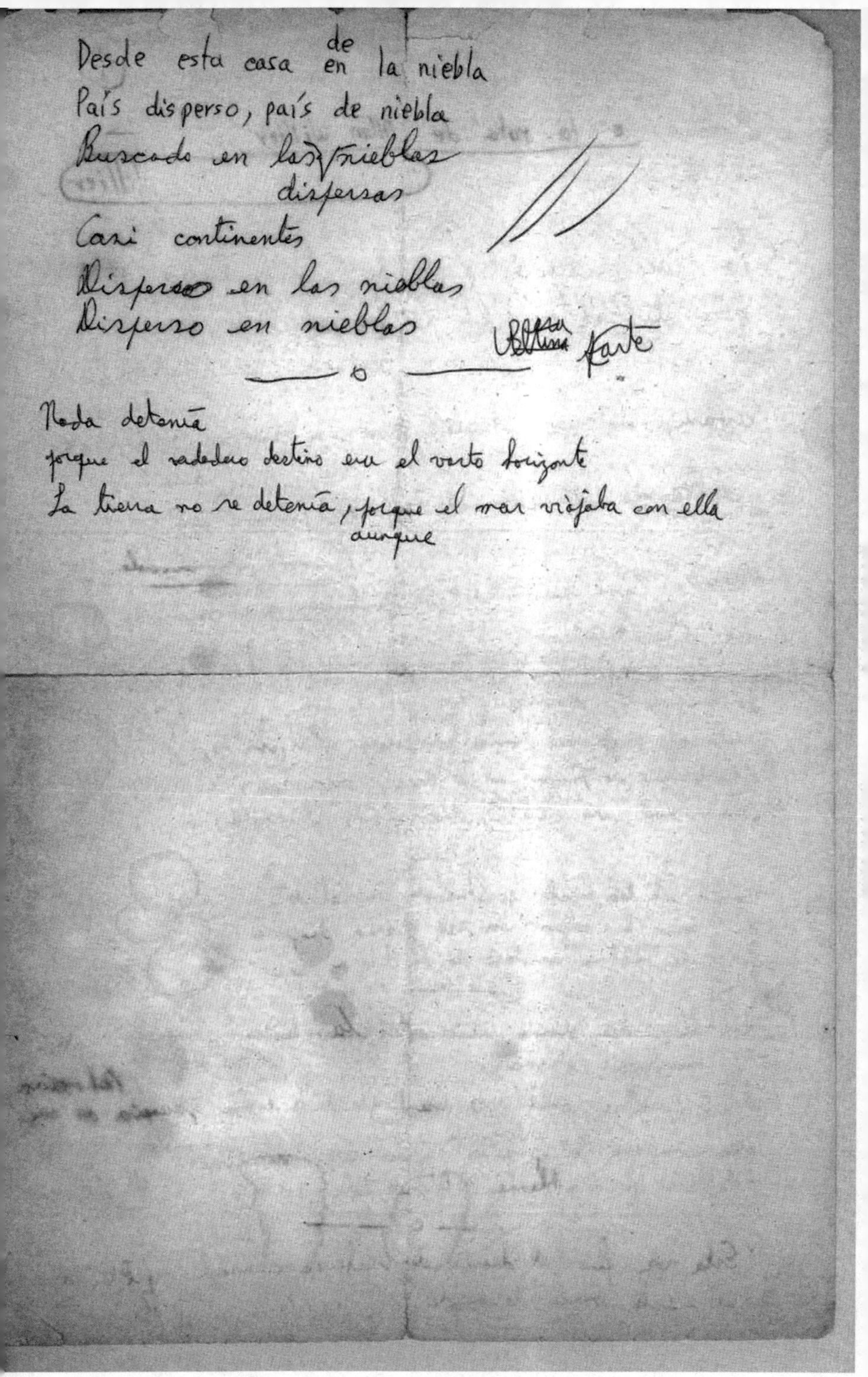

de
Desde esta casa en la niebla
País disperso, país de niebla
Buscado en las nieblas
dispersas
Casi continentes
Dispersos en las nieblas
Disperso en nieblas   Última Parte

— o —

Nada detenía
porque el verdadero destino era el vasto horizonte
La tierra no se detenía, porque el mar viajaba con ella
aunque

Draft of "The Face on the Bow, or the route of Allan Williers" pg.2

The Face on the Bow, or the Route of Allan Williers

And after the arrival of winter,
a morning filled with a sweet ash,
desolately solitary, seeking something lost in memory,
the last vagabond lost among the corners of a house
adrift and silent.
to finally stumble upon the face lost deep within a book.

“ . . . and I still remember my youth
and the feeling that will never come back anymore . . . ”

Joseph Conrad then emerged from a hidden space,
the summer landscape through a half-open window,
the twilight streets of the city resting on its docks
with snow that lit up and bloomed on the dead trees.
In those solitary hours, the word was nourishment,
a migratory dream made from its own substance
like a summoned sky taking various shapes,
the gloomiest day, the most secret rain,
the warmest nook at the edge of the world,
the pristine air of the rover of latitudes,
the incorrigible traveler over the seas of the East.

Then his hazy face came forth from the shadows,
springing from the wood with clear outlines
of a hand fashioning a compact memory,
a transparent fruit to gaze upon a tree,
a tender, perfumed heart at its center
like a single lamp on the bow of a ship.

And so one day Allan Williers set out to sea,
toward ancient, secretive kingdoms.
With eyes skimming a fleeing sky,
he was a man absorbed in his seafaring home,
his own voice calling from other shores
through the mist like in a waking dream,
with that sleeping face among the stars returning to its domain,
toward all distant lands yet to be revealed
and the tallest stars with their trembling cold.

Between waves like columns or cathedrals,
falling into the deepest abysses of the sea
against the still sky, three masts shone
creaking with power in a thick liquid of pulpy trees,
searching for the strange land of the skuas,
the dark birds that foresee death,
or beneath the luminous flight of the albatross,
made of the same mighty matter as wind and water,
that water, so cold, it "hurt and burned like fire."
A spirited steed was the white masts and spars,
breaking the strained air and the roars of glaciers
shattering with a tremor that flooded even the gray clouds
in its unwavering course,
the damp, unmoving figurehead
where silence makes no sense,
while rounding Cape Horn Rock,
baptized so by a Dutch captain in memory of home.

Across the land swept a desolate white wind,
echoing in the salt and the dream of that absent face,

always toward the possibility of the horizon and its other signs,
in a sun from another time, over the scattered south
and its dwellers born from the light of the ice,
with endless sleep in their forest of beech,
along the routes of the Chilote canoes toward slow settlements,
resurrecting the ghosts of Caribbean buccaneers or Nordic lands,
and those left adrift seeking cities in the fog,
tracing the foam trails of feats on agave rafts
and forgotten muskets amidst the crash of storms,
down the slopes of those who returned with Robinson Crusoe,
the solitary of lost days of childhood,
reconstructing the entire route of José de Moraleda's dugout canoe,
the very one that would make us dream over his chart of the Great
 Island,
sailing as if through a night sky over submerged hills,
emerging from time, after a long slumber,
with Conrad's face as a lamp that pushed back the night
so that Allan Williers
could continue seeking the items that would join them eternally to
 the sea.

The Presence of Something Ancestral: On Translating *Migratory Poems*

Mary Ann Christensen

WORKING ON *POEMAS MIGRATORIOS* was a rare opportunity to revisit a landscape I left almost nine years ago. I am grateful that I had some first-hand knowledge of the subject matter and was able to use my upbringing as a resource. These poems are steeped in images of the sea, wind and desolation as well as the presence of something ancestral within that loneliness. Cárdenas uses rhythm and silences to depict this landscape; I did not have to imagine it because I recognize it from memory.

The first step of translation was one I did quite pragmatically. I simply translated word for word, with no account for rhythm, imagery or any other poetic devices. I turned the poems to English very mechanically, barely thinking about it. But once this was achieved I took a great pause to read the original and then my crude translation.

By far, my largest aim was to pay tribute to the atmosphere created by Cárdenas.

In order to achieve this, I had to choose what to sacrifice. Because something had to be sacrificed, I cannot see another way to get a message across. On occasion, it was word choice—changing an adjective or an adverb here or there that was somewhat further removed from the original term—but that created an alliteration that worked, or had a connotation that further evoked Cárdenas' imagery.

There were times where I decided that the trade-off was to have no trade-off. That some elements, usually ones relating to nature and the naming of it, should remain in Spanish and I needed to contextualize the words surrounding it. Finding the English equivalent sometimes meant travelling too close to the realm of species and genus and it all felt too scientific. I often reached out to my big brother—a tour guide who holds a deep knowledge of birds and trees from the south of Chile, specifically Chiloé and Patagonia. He helped me find the middle ground between the indigenous, common, and scientific names, which otherwise might have distracted greatly from the poems. We texted back and forth between seven thousand miles and a four-hour time difference and he reminded me of words and names that I had forgotten in the time and distance between us that were brought back to me during this venture.

When It Is the Countryside Itself We Are Searching For, Part Two

An Interview with Jorge Aravena Llanca and Felipe Acevedo Riquelme

Translated by Daniela Anaís Jara Guevara and Valentina Merino Amigo. Berlin, Germany, 17 October 2024.

Felipe: Was there any difference between the relationship you and Rolando had as friends and the one you had as artists?

Jorge: In many aspects, we had different educations and different knowledge gaps. Rolando was an expert reader in universal poetry. He especially loved German poetry from the beginning of the 19th and 20th centuries, the poems of those who lived before, during, and after World War I. He had an advantage—above all creative—during these conversations, and his wisdom was always immediately apparent to everyone he spoke to. He was way ahead of many literature professors in terms of knowing even the smallest details of life that live in poetry, which was the inspiration, the source, the cause of all his imagery.

As friends? It was something different. Although I would remain silent and deferential while we were talking about poetry, in the more recreational spaces we both were chatty, fun. He loved to reminisce, and he loved to joke about his reminiscing.

I will tell you some funny things about Rolando and our friends. Rolando was devoted to creating axioms. He would always arrive at the Sociedad de Escritores de Chile[23] (SECH by its acronym in Spanish) with some of them that would soon linger in the memory of the writers of the bar Refugio López Velarde of the SECH, where we gathered every Tuesday until the first few hours of the early morning. Some of these axioms—same as some of Teillier's—were usually appropriated by Nicanor Parra, who had the habit of incorporating everything into his books. From Rolando, he took one of his expressions, which he would say out loud before going to the bathroom: "I will be right back." (trans.)[24] Nicanor took another phrase from Teillier that became popular around the world: "United States: the country where liberty is a statue." (trans.) [25] Another axiom Rolando was fond of, although not his: "In this holy place, where many people come, the most cowardly strains and the bravest shits their pants." (trans.) [26] This was frequently written on bathroom walls in Santiago. This, too, became a repeated anti-poem in the sponge-like mind of Nicanor Parra.

---

[23] Chilean Writers' Society

[24] Original: "Voy y vuelvo."

[25] Original: "En EEUU, la libertad es una estatua."

[26] Original: "En este lugar sagrado, donde viene tanta gente, hace fuerza el más cobarde y se caga el más valiente."

Felipe: What are the things that you admired the most about Rolando, as a person and as a poet?

Jorge: The love that he had for poetry, like a banner in a parade. His insatiability for books—he read everything his friends recommended, everything in their libraries. It was impossible for him to buy books. During his first years in Santiago, he would go to the Biblioteca Nacional[27] with a notebook in hand, request the books about poetry, and transcribe them for himself. One day he was doing exactly that when someone asked him what he was up to. Rolando showed them the book from which he had already transcribed various poems. This curious character was the poet Jorge Teillier, and this is how they met.

Teillier later added more to that story; it turned out that they both admired Georg Trakl, the poet who spoke with the dead: "we immediately got thirsty, and we stayed together for the night, with white wine, trying to end the production of all Chilean vineyards."

I believe it. This is also how my friendship with the two of them began.

Felipe: What do you think his poetry aimed (and still aims) to achieve?

Jorge: It still portrays the history of his era of the Magellanic South, but also the future of it. He found himself in that land. He sought his identity in the roots of the trees with thick trunks, branches, and leaves covered with snow, as well as in starving dogs and the busy streets—which were cold, whether

---

[27] National Library of Chile.

in the evening or in the always-descending nightfall. Rolando was a silent writer and a memorialist with an analytical and reserved look. What impacted him the most were the memories of his people, the surroundings, and the slowness of time. He once told me he was not searching for himself, but for the destiny of his ancestors.

He was not so different from Teillier. Both admired Trakl, Rilke, and other German poets such as Stefan George; and the French poets like Baudelaire, Voltaire, Gautier—the pioneer of Parnassianism—Flaubert, and Mallarmé; the American Edgar Allan Poe; Kant and Hegel on social matters; they also loved Schopenhauer and Nietzsche, especially Nietzsche. They were very knowledgeable about these thinkers—and many others—especially Chilean authors of their generation: Efraín Barquero, Óscar Hahn, Sergio Hernández, Armando Rubio, and Gonzalo Rojas. And of course, the two Pablos: Neruda and de Rokha.

Felipe: How do you think he approached life, and how did it evolve or change during the time you two knew each other?

Jorge: In his private life, Rolando was reserved and solitary. Even in Santiago, where the weather and social atmosphere are different, he remained the same solitary man walking through the snow. He lived in a boarding house between the streets of Cumming and Brasil, in a very neat and tidy little room. At the entrance you could immediately see a bookshelf filled with books—I estimated about 200—most of them were about poetry and history. There also were some novels. Each time I visited him I would read the spines without touching them and calculate the knowledge he had of them. He always referenced passages from books in his conversations.

By the look of his room, I think he was still in his homeland. There was only one bed, one table, and one tall, narrow wardrobe, where he kept the few clothes he had. He covered the few empty spaces on his walls with photos of the South—some from calendars. His furniture, although not much, took up almost all of the five square meters of his private refuge.

Felipe: To what extent was his worldview defined by his art?

Jorge: The solitude in which he lived defined both his life and his art. For him, it was never necessary to invite anyone into his room who was not a close friend. During the day, he worked a normal dayshift, thus the time he came back to his room was the moment to write, even if he was tired. He told me that this was when the words of his night readings would ripen, drink after drink with his friends. However intense it was, he would write without much difficulty. Wine every night at the SECH bar did not disturb his poetic divagations nor his manuscriptures. His penmenship was clear and straight, and his pages were tidy. He was well-balanced and confident about his thoughts. He rarely crossed out what he wrote, in his letters at least. I was fortunate that he sent me many of these—to Chillán,when I was working at the Universidad de Chile, to Ecuador when I lived there, and then to Berlin, Germany.

Felipe: The scenery is a huge force in his work. What did he think of his homeland? Did this change over time or did it get more complicated later in his life?

Jorge: I would say that he kept his sensibility and his capacity for observing the South intact. In spite of everything, it was very hard for him to go back. It was hard to know this about him unless you knew him well. In his everyday life, he seemed uncomplicated by place; he was concerned about people, nearly duty-bound to friendship. Though perhaps these were also ways of searching for something that was lost. This is similar to his memory of his father, who was a role model of integrity and decency for him. Rolando's work was honest; and despite the cold memories of his hometown, and the loneliness to which he had become accustomed, he remained a good and consistent friend.

Felipe: What do you think was the most important thing for him? How do you think he would have liked to be remembered? How do you think he would have liked people to read his work?

Jorge: I think the most important thing for him was friendship—the fact that he could lean on his close friends when he felt lonely and when he was missing his homeland, as well as close family members, and blood relatives. He was nostalgic, as his poems suggest. The contemplation of his faraway land was everpresent. Just like the one and only poet Trakl—who spoke with the dead—Rolando, for his part, had a small, green goblin from Chiloé in the eyelet of his fanciest jacket; he would even ask him for permission to stay longer in the bar and, at the same time, for protection—that someone would accompany him to his boarding house. Naturally, he believed in his poetry. I do not think there was anything romantic in the material scarcity of those small collections of poems.

Felipe: Do you have any stories about him writing poems or reflecting on his process?

Jorge: So many. He asked me to pay for the cost of printing copies of his poems, since he was very poor. His compositions were constant; he thought while he walked and even more when he was in the solitude of his room. I never saw, heard, or was told that he asked for feedback on his poetic reflections. I think he took it for granted that no matter how formal his style was, it was well regarded, and I am sure that he thought that by being part of the group and of that Generation of 1950, they were outstanding. This made him very confident and kept him writing poetry without much editing.

Rolando was a poem himself. He radiated poetry in his dress, his way of speaking with so much seriousness about the work of his friends, even while he kept quiet about his own. Many said, amongst themselves, that Rolando Cárdenas was more of a poet than Teillier: more profoundly reflective, not just about where he was from, but also the historic burden of it, the native peoples that disappeared and all the parents who died. He wrote about the creation of villages and not just about his own bohemian persona. He lovingly and sweetly matched his memories of his childhood with the love and dreams of his lost southern towns. He also suggested that his elders and fellow countrymen should make their "home their second bar" so as not to die of boredom.

From Berlin, on this first day of Fall in 2024, I am so far from the streets we walked together, the cold sunrises of our returns home. I felt then and now that the company of a friend was more significant than any origin-less crowd, who knows not where they are going. I grew thanks to his friendship, and realized that life with poetry and music is lighter and more sincere.

Felipe: Were you familiar with his creative process?

Jorge: Not completely. That was a solitary practice. I think as a friend I offered a stable and quiet family life. I was someone who welcomed him into a peaceful home, overrun with children. They would also embrace Rolando when they saw him arrive, since even for children, he was lovingly dedicated and tender. His friends' girlfriends loved him, even if they saw him leaving at the end of his visits, talking with his Green Goblins about who knows what poems.

When it came to writing his poems, he was very reserved. However, with friends he radiated joy, even when he recited his poetry in front of an audience. Also, I believe I am one of the few to whom he introduced Sonia, his official girlfriend. She is in a picture I took with Teillier on our way to La Serena many decades ago. She still writes to me and greets me with memories of Rolando.

When it came to women, Rolando was a mystery. He never gave signs of being in a relationship, nor was he really ever seen dating someone. Conversely, he was always surrounded by poetesses who evidently loved him and lavished attention on him; he confessed this to me one day when we were heavily drinking. That same day, I accompanied Rolando on one of his dates, to the door of a woman he was hiding. We passed through the Plaza de Armas,[28] we arrived at a certain address, a certain floor, and a certain door. He said goodbye enthusiastically, meaning for me to leave immediately.

[28] The main square of Santiago.

When the door opened, a lady appeared: the beautiful Ester Matte Alessandri, niece of Arturo Alessandri, who had been president of Chile. It turns out, she was hiding him more than he was hiding her!

A lyrical baritone, Rolando used to play the guitar and sing. He'd studied choral music, and his voice was sonorous and well-trained. This made him popular with his friends when they'd been drinking—but also elsewhere. He was invited to be a soloist in the choir of the Universidad Técnica de Santiago, where he studied and graduated as a construction engineer, as far as I remember. He later worked in a CORFO[29] agency office.

He arrived in Santiago with his guitar, which only in his hands sounded beautiful, and a treasure of songs about his homeland. He played a beautiful waltz from Chiloé or Punta Arenas, which he sometimes played as a *tonada*[30] called "Corazón de escarcha." Unfortunately, a well-known singer, the Chilean folklorist Héctor Pavez, copied this song from him, which launched his career. Héctor was never invited to the community because of this action, that is a fact.

Felipe: Do you think Cárdenas' work as a poet was affected by the military coup of 1973 and the later dictatorship? How did it affect him as a person and as an artist?

Jorge: Absolutely, the dictatorship affected him, in the same way it did many others. It was terrible for him, how the censorship impacted him, with such ignorance to the benefits of his work and its place in Chilean literature. That was the point; the military dictatorship was carried out to kill Chilean

---

[29] CORFO is a local office of the Production Development Corporation, which sought to make Chile a more developed nation.

[30] A folkloric Chilean song style.

intelligence. It slowly killed Rolando; he was dismissed from his job as a construction engineer, and he was never hired again in any public office. He could not find work, and was forced to live off the generosity of his friends and what little money he could make by selling photocopies of his poems.

His ending was very sad. He died in absolute poverty. His partner Eliana "Nana" Oyarzo had died, and he continued living in her apartment, without the consent of her family. The apartment was besieged by Nana's nephews and the police, who wanted him gone. In Berlin, I received plenty of letters from Rolando, which I have since donated to the Biblioteca Nacional. He shared the troubling facts of his hardship—how couldn't even afford to continue feeding his cat. He asked me for help so he could survive.

When he did die, there was a massive turnout for his funeral, so large it was considered an anti-dictatorship protest.

The rest of his sad end is described by Ramón Díaz Eterovic. How Ramón, noticing that Rolando's lifeless body was without his famous tie, took his own off and placed it firmly on the neck of his friend.

His soul, in his lifetime, had been so full of hope. And his end was lonesome, dislocated, agonized. You do not see this in his poems, you only see the brilliant future. This brilliant light is what he left us: himself, his southern homeland. He gave us this as a friend, and, even moreso, he gave us this as a poet.

What, Behind Those Walls, 1986

Translated by Mathew Weitman

What, Behind Those Walls

From outside, such intrigues:
who lives in the diffuse light
of the indeterminate lamp—
who still dines among us, who is not here.

Who are the residents beyond the curtains,
prolonging our dreams by pouring bee-silence
into a grand ritual of redness.

What behind those walls stops our steps.

Any room is strange enough to fertilize us with its mystery:
something more must happen
than the simple complicity of night—
bodies, faces, & hands seal this discovery deep inside the walls
that protect them, in the table that perfumes them.

The absent ones are fierce behind those walls:
welcome is he who returns to find his bed again.

All the seasons are like unknowable houses:
the abstract presence of keys, of windows, of doors
are insurmountable walls—
walls to keep from desecrating the lives beyond them.

What, behind those walls,
thickens to guard an obstinate & invincible intimacy.

Doors

What, behind those doors.
How many doors is this house made of—
doors wide open, half-open, & unopen
upon the distinct solemn beauty of each beloved face.

Once, we were introduced through a mysterious door.
We rebuilt it confusedly
—almost absently—
one unique & terrible day
unlike any other.

The beginning of childhood
was imprisoned behind the wood.

But how many doors are our lives made of:
how much material must inundate us
before we are accustomed to them,
know them as the owners of secrets,
& simultaneous visitors.

The sky is too dizzying for its inhabitants to remain there:
strangers searching for strangers to meet again
in different worlds,
between foreign doors.

Everyone is a diner behind this door.
This door is a table for those who lost their dreams
—naked, beaten, wet bodies—
angels listen & protect them.

We'll close our door to no one.
It will be forever promising to the call—
to the days of long & devouring light,
to the blind nights that consume us like dark earth.

Clock, the Tired Face of the House

What silence fills this house.
In it, the old clock is the tired face of time:
an ancient gentleman dozing through the afternoon.

We are protected by his stillness,
but this guardian disturbs us with his determined presence—
points to us with his cyclical eye from everywhere
as if from some unseen shore.

The sun is already old when we see it for the first time
& the night is naïve when we—
the simultaneous inhabitants & prisoners
of its imperturbable rhythm—
finally notice it.

Today, the fragile snow
reminds us of the slow rush of blood
as it falls with the starlight
for hours. We've gotten used to it.

Time is silent in its sphere
where Death does not rise
& our lives are like fruits that never rot.
The end & the beginning are a singular vastness
collected by numbers
in a solitary circle.

What a strange way to mark our steps:
this simple & terrible terrestrial object,
in the quiet of the house,
with its tired face.

Floors, Creaking

At night, places change
& sounds sicken even
the most sanctioned ears.

Everything is full of earth: torrents of dirt
cover & crunch down upon us
until we disappear, like apples.

The sound of wood shifting in the night:
when no one touches it,
when no one harms it.

The darkness searches for us—
surprises us: magically shows
us that we are passing through it.

& we hear the wooden sound,
in spite of this change.

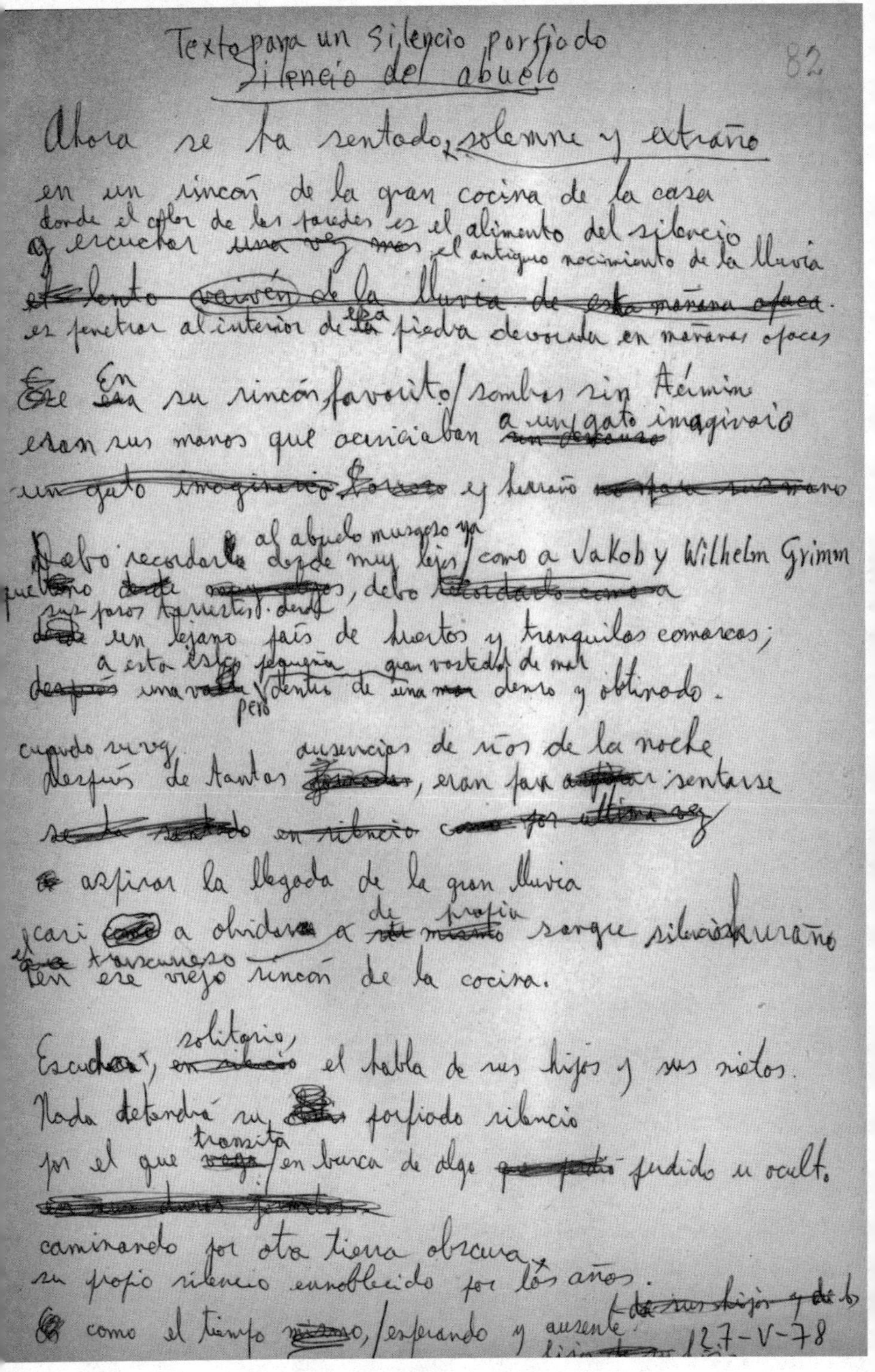
Texto para un silencio porfiado
~~Silencio del abuelo~~

82

Ahora se ha sentado, solemne y extraño
en un rincón de la gran cocina de la casa
donde el color de las paredes es el alimento del silencio
y escuchar ~~una vez más~~ el antiguo nacimiento de la lluvia
~~el lento vaivén de la lluvia de esta mañana opaca.~~
es penetrar al interior de esa piedra devorada en mañanas opacas

En esa su rincón favorito / sombras sin término
eran sus manos que acariciaban a un gato imaginario
~~un gato imaginario~~ y huraño

Debo recordarlo al abuelo musgoso ya desde muy lejos / como a Jakob y Wilhelm Grimm
pueblerino, debo
sus pasos terrestres
un lejano país de huertos y tranquilas comarcas;
a esta pequeña gran vastedad de mar
una pero dentro de una denso y obstinado.

cuando su vez ausencias de ríos de la noche
Después de tantas, eran para sentarse
~~se ha sentado~~ en silencio ~~como por última vez~~

aspirar la llegada de la gran lluvia
casi a olvidarse a de propia porque silencio huraño
el trascurso
en ese viejo rincón de la cocina.

Escuchar, solitario, ~~en silencio~~ el habla de sus hijos y sus nietos.
Nada detendrá su porfiado silencio
por el que transita en busca de algo perdido u oculto.

caminando por otra tierra obscura,
su propio silencio ennoblecido por los años.
como el tiempo, esperando y ausente ~~de sus hijos y de los~~
12-V-78

Early draft of "Now He Sits, Solemn & Strange."

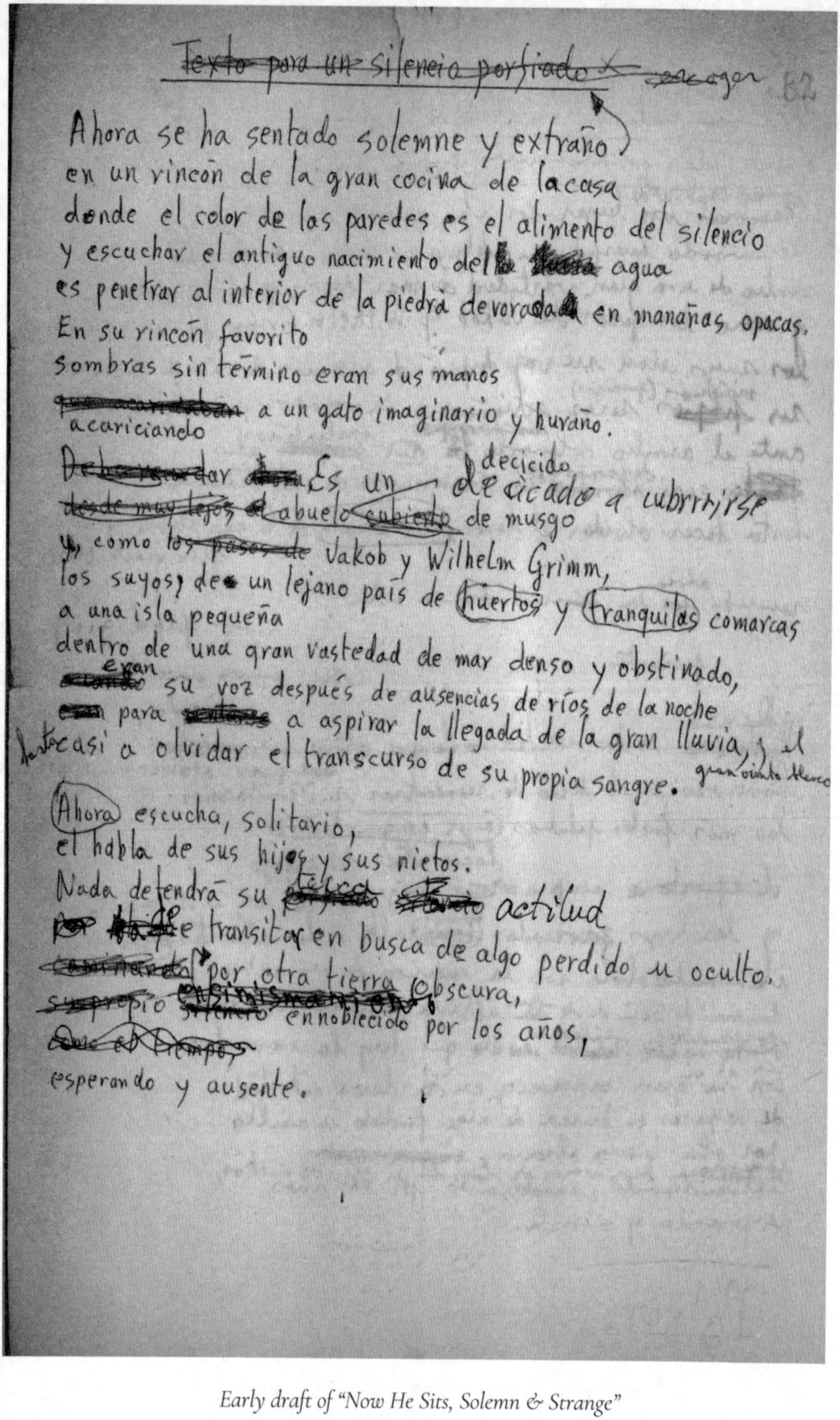
~~Texto para un silencio porfiado~~ x ~~escoger~~ 82

Ahora se ha sentado solemne y extraño
en un rincón de la gran cocina de la casa
donde el color de las paredes es el alimento del silencio
y escuchar el antiguo nacimiento del ~~[illegible]~~ agua
es penetrar al interior de la piedra devorada en mañanas opacas.
En su rincón favorito
sombras sin término eran sus manos
~~que acariciaban~~ acariciando a un gato imaginario y huraño.
~~Debe guardar~~ ~~[illegible]~~ Es un decidido dedicado a cubrrrirse
~~desde muy lejos~~ el abuelo ~~cubierto~~ de musgo
y, como ~~los pasos de~~ Jakob y Wilhelm Grimm,
los suyos, de un lejano país de huertos y tranquilas comarcas
a una isla pequeña
dentro de una gran vastedad de mar denso y obstinado,
~~[illegible]~~ eran su voz después de ausencias de ríos de la noche
~~[illegible]~~ para ~~[illegible]~~ a aspirar la llegada de la gran lluvia, y el gran viento blanco
hasta casi a olvidar el transcurso de su propia sangre.

Ahora escucha, solitario,
el habla de sus hijos y sus nietos.
Nada defendrá su terca ~~[illegible]~~ ~~[illegible]~~ actitud
~~[illegible]~~ de transitar en busca de algo perdido u oculto.
~~caminando~~ por otra tierra obscura,
~~su propio silencio~~ ennoblecido por los años,
~~[illegible]~~
esperando y ausente.

Early draft of "Now He Sits, Solemn & Strange"

Now He Sits, Solemn & Strange

Now he sits solemn & strange
in the corner of the house's grand kitchen
where the color of the walls
is the food of silence, listening to the ancient sound
of water's birth penetrating the inside of a stone—
devouring it in the opacity of morning.

Long ago, he decided to cover his clothing with moss
& change places with someone else, to disappear:
a recriminated guest thinning his shadow
in the dense maritime vastness; obstinate
as the Brothers Grimm, whose voices are like the absent rivers
of night tirelessly invoking mythical beings
to our amazement on instantaneous wings,
almost unaware of their own blood's progeny—
forgetting the fear of great rains & white winds.

This desire to rediscover ancestral ties is overwhelming:
the most faithful words are in the back of the mirror
recovering faces. Again, the journey:
the long walk toward our relatives
illuminated now by an emerging star.

Almost foreign since his last stay, an astonished quiet
envelopes him today: his great fatigue,
his enigmatic patriarchal demeanor,
like someone returning in search of some lost or hidden thing
from some other dark world, to listen to the voices
of his children & grandchildren—
ennobled by his years,
waiting & absent.

In Immediate Absence, the Birth of Alba

Someone slips silently against me
in the secret sleeping night.

As the earth turns, we turn together, slowly.
We dive into the sweet dense waters,
into a vast nocturnal ocean.

Someone slips through this winter-facing house
imperceptible as Rumor,
without disturbing the deep call of a dream
traveling through the unexplored universe
toward a more enigmatic silence:
this zone, oscillating between shadow
& lamplight, like the foliage of trees
at night, renews the softness
of your brilliant skin.

Behind these walls
there is something that never stops passing:
a propitious solitude for flowing blood—
or your southern face meeting mine
& covering me.

This is the room that detains me among its objects,
& this is the door that guards my sleeping face.

After this: after leaving
the house where I always forget something
with the help of memory, I will return
to you & stop myself again
before the invocation of your door
—held ajar by my silent & secret requests—
& you will slip behind it,
against me.

A Tree is the Center of the World

There are beings inside me—
beings in all places of the night
too dark for the illumination of snow.
The snow whitens & buries everything
magnificent & stubborn.

How many absences must I recognize
beneath this frozen meadow,
where taciturn passersby hurry along.
They live in this silent place
where a tree is the center of the world:
a tall leafy signal of the chosen spot
where they winter with their relatives,
where they're devoured by dreams.

I'll wait for them in the doorway of this same house,
where they reconvene with their past lives—
willingly dispensing of themselves
in the same distinct ways: leaving
their empty chairs, their untouched utensils.
& emerging from their white covers
they recognize themselves in the likeness
of their deep rootedness, in the faithful
reconstruction of their steps—
feeling them from beyond
an insurmountable wall on a distant shore,
without gestures, without words.

Their endlessness only astonishes
those who still breathe & dream
in this house of return.

Revelation of the Snow

How many bells do we remember ringing in the
graveyard:
absently, they've lived with us since yesterday
—today & tomorrow—
like the taste of some fruit
we've never gotten used to.

But the snow will reveal
the unburied, the exiled,
those who—like us—wander
with lightning & ire, without measuring
the confines of their strange rooms,
without completing their nightly rounds,
& their days of rose-colored winds—
without completing the small yet perfect circle
in which they most feel the ownership
of their blood's accustomed movement.

The earth turns:
this is the inexorable law that keeps us
from each other. We're astonished
to recognize the day as the day
& the night as the most disturbing part
of the world: it returns to us over & over again,
helps us die with its invisible force,
timidly lucid. At the same time,
something marks us—something disquieting,
like a deep calling voice that transforms
everything into a white song.

We always ask the snow
—eternal & strange—
to reveal its secrets:
beneath it, we find
every face we've ever loved.

No One Cares About Your Intimate Visions Brought On by Doubt

How we live on echoless returns—
hanging in a vertiginous space,
unable to stop our Seven League Boots.

The wind now, for example, gathers the voices
& faces we spent today in search of:
there is a street that appears & disappears in memory,
but finds no foothold in the presence of the sea or hills.
& there is a house we have similarly misunderstood—
the lives inside it aren't our concern.
Its doors, its windows, its red roof
remind us of something we can't quite name—
something that left too quickly,
or maybe we've simply been detained for too long.

We need to find the face
in the mirror that once captured us,
but suddenly we're returning—
joylessly separated like a secret kept by Death.

We wanted to stop time from slipping
through our hands on senseless streets.
The voiceless words, the wind-spun trees
had a name once & inhabited Today.
But a burning log
from the land of bonfires
removes us from the white city.

A Fuegian Woman, Memories of Now

You cannot return to the silent past:
today, you belong to memory.
No other islands sail behind you:
you are an unburied continent.

Legitimate flower, tumultuous waters:
inheritance of the sea's white sand.
Stolen stars, petrified hills:
cheekbones cruelly carved by wind.

Snow flees guanaco skin:
bedspreads scaring off the night.
Tremulous foliage: awaiting old mornings.

A hardened face full of frozen earth.
A grey bird cawing: sky's wind.
Sphynx of southern stone: you no longer exist.

Samuel Donoso

Y el vino corría ligero como un alguacil
—Juan Ruiz

Naked in the wind & lonely
you were intent on returning
to the same shore, where
wine flowed lightly like a bailiff.

From lightning light
to rain & sun: your silence
is compacted in your mineral roots,
your earthly misadventures.

From the tenacious work of inscription
—succinct engravings in stone & metal—
you sought to become dilapidated corners:
shadows erased the profile
of your face & your dreams—
El dulce misterio de la vida
that you did not find in your haste.

How it marks our soul,
this wine we drink in your memory:
this wine I search for beneath every light—
making you transparent, bit by bit.
Surely you were smiling when you said goodbye,
waving your handkerchief in the air—
asking only to be a happy memory,
to remain the party's heart.

Climates

I.
Which powerful flash of snow will we conserve
in our memory as the supreme winter—
not the fearful deathward crashing of a runaway horse,
not the last perfume of sunset falling on the roses
of the house. Before the vast whitened prairies
are illuminated again for many long years,
I will quietly say, *those small falling feathers*
disperse the course of our dreams: they are vestiges
fused together by the frost & voyage of morning.

It is a long meridian night in the lonely canals below
as they await the tenderness of this hour
like wide rivers already matured
—as if their rising waters were in search of their designs—
or like a sheep silently breathing beneath great sheets
of light, feeding itself on the endless chain of its own wool;
or like the capsized ships of fisherman who won't return
with empty nets in a single explosion
of terrible beauty, or expectant vigils for everyone
who has ever been astonished by the broken sky
wandering without rising—never appearing
with the enormity of its small burnt trees pointing accusingly
in the direction beyond the ocean,
like a connoisseur of discrete expeditions
in which the whole of Nature moves unmoored—
unrenouncing & unrelenting, restlessly awaiting
the completion of another cycle.

II.

The entire province is subjected to the frequent enormous silences
of autumn, despite the ancient bonfires
transmitting legends of great emerald empires
& kingdoms where man was reborn in the secret of water,
or reached profound exhaustion in the mountains,
the clouds, & the red stars traversing the night.

The wide avenues of sky
& the capricious wide furrows in the earth
—this is the season!—
open with the sonorous wingbeats of migratory birds
as the trees redden with slow atavistic beards:
time descends from poor wooden fences,
a lonely drop of moisture drawn from a window
falls melancholically from a red roof:
fog-hung streets: distant white city without noise,
almost noiseless through the crossing's hard needles.

The peninsula is surrounded
by the purest shores: porticos of aging men
cared for by their solitude & the schedule of the plains
—their forlorn old prints of sheep, & horses, & dogs—
guided only by the astral sign of Aldebaran piercing the dark,
wrapped in the tender perfume of *coirón* & wet earth,
watched through the rain by the penetrating eye of the *calafate*
that wants to wash its abstracted heart
without the last bird of the season: the breeze of its exile
reaches the gray day's distant shores,
& in the chaste language of permanent absences
this vast space of sky & earth is not ruled by the leaves.

III.
The sun today is a slow enigma:
spring's thickets of the first bird's eggs
—in another time, the trees did not hold them.
Now is the time to build canoes: now is the time
for the guanacos to return to the mountains,
for the black-faced ibis & partridges to prepare to fly.

The sky's dawn is an immense & immemorial region
reflecting unmoving hamlets & errant flocks:
ghostly ships made of peaceful fleeces, pushed along by foehns
—the ground below: a table set for the late arriving guests.
The brilliance of the first wild strawberries shine with dew:
glimpses of small coral islets quickly disappear.
In the force of the sun, everything changes—
the sleeping minerals transform; hit by its fire, the oceanic wind
lifts the perfume of vegetables from their depths
& opens the drafty iridescent caves with a golden key.

Nothing is left to chance:
the moss surrounding the house is dense:
a green knot that breaks the wintered silence.
Nothing is still nor strange to Fertility,
his seed sowing spell
moves men to pick up their farm tools
& shake the mosquitos from their propitious harvests
as they prepare the horses & tills for a long cropping.
Everything is accompanied by a faint sound of growth & pine-
smell,
memory grafts itself to the seedbeds
as hands ascend from the earth, refertilized.

IV.
& in the longest days of the year
this house sits in the light of all hours.
What name to give summer's clarity:
what name to give the small night's afterglow.
The sky will be the mirror's violent desire:
in it, we will see a transparent earth
—a set table at the edge of the world,
with victuals & goblets of the highest order—
like the heron's way of scratching space,
like the fish who longs to glimpse the air above.

The long ocean, rippling & enormous,
cannot stop breathing long enough to be still.
Now, it wants to travel to the city—
visit all the houses:
a tempestuous fugitive, an abstracted visitor
in the plains, like an old man known by his beasts,
in his hills of *coirón* where he lost his horse.
The city
—with its red rooftops & greens grayed by ancient rains—
happily descends from the hills to the shores,
crossed only by the thin dark sheet of the Las Minas River.

What to do with those days in the memory of long whitened nights
curving quickly toward frozen continents,
where we knew birds fluttered in the naked air until it was late,
& there were almost no shadows in the silent bedrooms
where our own shadows linger: today is all we have.

Stanzas for George Trakl, Poet of the Dead

1.
In the serene spring of our country
we greet each vigorous year in the orchards
with the delight of wine.
Now, it is time for the farmer's work song
to converse with the land,
time for his tools to excavate its secrets:
harmless, he must know about the migratory birds
as his crops silently burst open in the afternoon.

A stove illuminates the greedy faces of girls
& young men who hide the strength of their blood—
they move away from the rooster's waking
ignoring the chaffs of wheat,
the deer dying in the forest.

It is the village
where the night's wind disperses the unreal world.
Everyone is distant & tender,
like the first sled weaving through the birch trees,
or the songs of the rosary:
& I love you, Rustic Washerwoman—
wherever you go you carry the somber autumn
of childhood, the faint smell of mignonette,
images of a pond breaking, & a silent sleepy cat
eclipsing the moon.

In the village,
time is calm as a dead child.

2.
« Verflossen ist das Gold der Tage »
There is white water to drink from the pond beneath the
willows
when we are thirsty.

The evening poppy is an angel in the dark city.

Gretl's letter remembers the sad melody
sung at the foot of the soldier's soul.

You emerge from the autumnal landscape as a torrent
of blood absorbed in words—
desolate as the suffering of white walls hidden beneath a roof
that spurns even the moon's clarity:
pale adolescents regarding one another with anxious arms.

3.
Now, the dark days of walnut trees
beneath the eyelid's pinkening of the seasons,
the rhythmic gestures of our hands stop.

This happened once long ago—
in the time of sand dunes & indecipherable dreams,
the time of suicides & battles with unburied faces,
the time of lost flocks in frigid waters.

In the smooth calm of autumn 72 years ago,
fearful questions were asked about the tavern's decrepit beams.

Goodbye to ancient legends of evil's dilated eye—
the soft dew on childhood's gray
grapes placed beside the bread.

Goodbye to snow on the windowsill, on the table
that provides for us—goodbye to the soul
moaning sweetly beside another heart.

The time of crows & hazelnuts is broken
by a herd of black & bay horses.

Atrás, green hunters, brimming with cruelty & madness.
Atrás, you small sonata of animals in the foliage.
Atrás, fishermen of the great black fish's fragile lineage.

Naked,
in a red boat
& far from the ritual of searching
for ancient apples,
you will leave, tremulous
as a hand in the act of killing.

The interminable night will not come.

November third, 1914:
never more
will evil stop on the ruined staircase
of the paternal house.

My Intimate Visions Brought on by Doubt: On Translating *What, Behind Those Walls*

Mathew Weitman

QUE, *TRAS ESOS MUROS*, the final volume of poetry Rolando Cárdenas would live to see published in his all-too-brief career, is filled with the most mature iterations of his most enduring lyrical motifs: friendship, ancestral memory, and the vastly contrasting landscapes of Santiago and Punta Arenas. With this, I do not mean to suggest that one can track the refinement of some inchoate themes first explored in *Tránsito Breve* that are finally "realized" in his final collections; but rather, with *Que, Tras Esos Muros* comes an almost abrupt shift in Cárdenas's sensibility as a poet. Though his subjects remain the same well-worn sites of lyric inquiry, they are marked by a newfound poignancy. Gone the sound of clinking glasses and the laughter of friends; instead, the empty table. Gone are the faces of our beloveds, buried beneath the snow.

Throughout this collection—Cárdenas's first in over a decade, and his first of the Pinochet regime[28]—the speaker of these poems is often suspended in liminal spaces: in the disused houses of myth and memory; between the steps of Seven League Boots. Our ancestors return but are almost unrecognizable—as mythical as a tale retold by The Brothers Grimm. The genocide of the civilizations before us—the Fuegians, the Selk 'Nam—serve as important reminders of a silent colonial past we've never escaped. The guanacos return to the hills, the old taverns fall apart, the red roofs of the city remind us of something we can't quite name. The only constant is the seasons: an expected change that never fails to surprise us.

While not overtly political, I could never shake the feeling that the poems in *Que, Tras Esos Muros* are especially coded, charged with censorship, knowingly enciphered. In these translations, I have sought to highlight such suggestions without sacrificing the brilliance with which Cárdenas obscures them. For example, in my translation of "In Immediate Absence, the Birth of Alba," I have translated the phrase "Este es la estancia que me retiene . . . " (literally:[29] "This is the room that *retains* or *keeps* me . . .") as "This is the room that *detains* me . . . " to signal Cárdenas's possible allusion to his own detainment in the Chilean National Stadium turned detention center in 1973. Similarly, in "The Revelation of Snow," I have translated "sin

---

[28] Though *Poemas Migratorios* was published in 1974, it was selected as the winner of the prestigious Pedro de Oña Award in 1972 (less than a year before the September 11th military coup). One can deduce that the two-year gulf between this honor and the book's ensuing self-publication was a consequence of the Pinochet regime.

[29] I don't mean to suggest here that a "literal" translation is ever possible but only to illustrate how my process differs from the more exacting translations of someone like Vladimir Nabokov.

medir los limites de su extraña habitación" (literally: "without measuring the *limits* of their strange rooms") to "Without measuring the *confines* of their strange rooms."

Despite the tonal shift of *Que, Tras Esos Muros*, formally, these poems remain characteristically Cárdenasian: images accrue with parataxis, breath is the measure of every line. While I have made minor changes to stanzaic length, punctuation, and—in very few cases—the order of certain images, I have done my best to preserve the flowing syntax of these poems (the colon and the em dash being my tools of choice). As such, these translations are my best attempts to bring forth the music of Rolando Cárdenas by prioritizing the singularity of his poetics: the *coirón* remains *coirón*, the *calafate* remains *calafate*; the words of Juan Ruiz and George Trakl remain in—or, in the case of the latter, "return to"—their original languages. The dark river is more explicitly the Las Minas, but the white city is never named.

Vast Empires, 1994

Translated by María Paz Wallffiguer Mardones

Talking Across Distant Hills

We have seen and dwelled much sea,
contemplating from high hills
colored by the trees. They say
it is good to recall the blue of the waters
when it is blue, and we name
friends holed up in some bar,
pirates mending pipes,
for they know nothing else
but to withdraw from their dreams by drinking.

I see only the hills and remark
that the harsh wine is distant and kind.
You listen in silence on the wide plain.
We wait to delight
in this autumn's time, talking of everything
with the clearest voice
that echoes in the fullness
of your silence and my parched throat,
thinking about our coming return
to the paradise of family and friends.

Of Praise and Albatrosses

Of praise and albatrosses we are made,
nocturnal bonfires, dreams and ships,
stones and lands of coirón, great temples of the wind.
Eternal works of sailors overtaken by the sea.
There are peaks, seen from the
highest gathering of waters,
shaped during the earth's passage,
strange land of skuas,
birds that divine death,
we are made.

After the arrival of that sweet ash,
prowling atavistic visions of nocturnal gardens
with knowledge of that water so cold
it "hurt and burned like fire," [30]
of praise and feverish seabirds
we are made,
eternal virtue of a figurehead.

---

[30] "dolía e quemaba como fuego" from the original text of "El descubrimiento del Estrecho de Magallanes" (The Discovery of the Strait of Magellan) by the Reverend P. Pablo Pastells (1920, Madrid, Spain), as cited in the original poem of Rolando Cárdenas in *Obras Completas.*

Happy Farmers

But the strange foreigners are still there,
aking away the expanse of waters,
to say the least,
our vast empires,
the narrow bed
created for great desires,
parties in the big city
far from the high sea breath, its borders
Troy-like deserved.

Having accepted the challenge,
we are renewed with our banners
without yielding from nights, dunes, and spring tides
traceless delights for your face
of brackish ebbs and hives of nocturnal fear
now, unabashedly recalling that sour wine,
ruddy red, crowned with melodies,
climbing and descending wire fences,
we were happy farmers
through fields without the fullness of the moonlight.

Visible Signs

From within the distance,
we will return to the fruits
stored in the favorable corner.
Nothing changes in the house.
The sun sheds its light every day,
always a new skin to touch.
Messenger of good fortune, it comes and goes
and falls asleep in its rhythm,
in its deepest folds,
to keep untouched the sleep of its beings.

We are dwellers of its presence,
a memory of earth or damp wood
full of its fruitfulness,
vigil for regions and murmurs of nocturnal trees.

But a visible sign is the absence.
In your new room,
it is nourishment.

Herons

What color fills the day
when the heron, slender stem, is above the water,
and below its own reflection.

The afternoon is a pause
from its own pleasant descent, gentle of neck,
exile and intoxication, golden scattered clouds.

That happens in the vast maritime provinces
frequented by coirón grasses
according to the hues the wind wishes to bestow
across hills until it finds new lagoons,
small oases populated by stubborn waters,
yet blue for the queens' repose.

Therefore, they are not even sings
that emerge from a constellation,
accusing them from afar,
nor do their flights pierce the air
spurred by harsh contrasts of arriving snow
or immature men.

Thus, they grow bored of their beauty
and their mysterious silence.

Snowing

It will be the purest garment chosen for you.
Owner without perennial shores, caves from above.
To descend, and descend again is her only will
without traced paths toward hidden mornings
without routes of the night,
her dark nakedness has also been discovered.

It is a splendid sight from above.
The city rising toward her foaming darts,
careened vessels, ghostly ships anchored
emerge with small forests and hidden birds,
houses, belongings, and inhabitants in their white dream
called to meet an unbidden sun
from that mansion descending, absorbing and beautiful
to softly take possession of promised destinies.

Clearly, in this unburied earthly city
its noble and ambitious treasures will be found
delights for visible generations
that will believe unwritten chronicles,
there are no borders nor smoky traces
to reign with majesty across its expanse.

Trough, or the Torment of Apples

We will necessarily dwell inside a barrel of apples
on a ship of enchantment and bewitched gifts
fleeing from the hoarse rum
toward beautiful countries of idyllic praise.

Lands of wood and ingenuity
prostrated before the arrogance of the feverish thirst
emerging from the pride of the hammer
altering the essence of a forest close
to times without quarrels, day and midnight,
next to horses and trade winds.

Bristly fields for candor
and the rough shape of the trough, inclined angle
toward upright rods for isochronous rhythms
that will perfume the air and remote skies
of succulent apples to carpet throats,
bubbling, tenacious light in dark doors, yet warm,
scattered by the generous joy of a different age,
fruit made nectar of its own mystery.

Birloche[31] Inland Towards the Sea

Quietly and loudly
we must murmur after centuries of journeys
that we must be at peace with the sea
of the ocean's man and the inland's
that emerge with their ghosts
and all their accompanying birds.

The continents may surface
like gigantic wandering whales
providing other geographies with their peculiar delights,
light and oil to the perennial wood.

Let us listen to the murmur of the groaning forest
clamoring for its shattered green mansions
by oxen forging the path of the birloche
recklessly breaking the horizons of its rooms
iceless sleigh or inexorable boat
seeking the sea with its wooden timber,
startling the contours
to reunite with the undertow or the spring tide
in this lament uttered among warriors
who will guard its gifts with noble bearing.

---

[31] "Birloche" is a type of sleigh or cart pulled by oxen used mostly on the Chiloé Island in southern Chile.

Exalting Bread

The far away countries visited
with the propitious thought
alert on the clearest mornings,
it will be time for joyful cypresses
on that side of the world
where the wind rises fiercely at night
and on lethargic days.

Lowly weeds among brambles of construction
debris with the scent of alfalfa
to breastfeed clay of its gestation
with a shy sun hidden in its dough
rising of the appetite of man's hunger
satisfied in his tray and generous tables
along all the bustling hillsides.
It is its hidden arrival in beer.

Now, therefore,
is the engrossed moment of exalting bread
before the land and the sea,
for it is said
that one day we will vanish between them both.

Ángela Lois Died Today

All could have been yesterday or always.
If you were not dead, you would die
from your own dream of fishing
south of stormy seas
among islands and cliffs that agreed
that the celebration of fire in their canoes
could not be held on any shore.

Omens of marine reapings without real dread
were announced by winged nocturnal companions
and executors describe without caciques,
land hunters, archers, nomads all at once
when they were with Ángela Lois
without relatives, like the few they were.

But they were already legends of great dispossessed ones,
hair parts for beautiful lineages of the earth,
An Ona, chief of the rainy south among mists.
That year of nineteen seventy-five
would end her people forever,
face carved by time, Ángela Lois
behind the space of lost Fuegian paths.

Floating Country

From the floating country
afternoon rosebushes,
vegetables and modest fruits,
the grandmother among ploughs,
her ancient nobility,
atavism of Chiloé.

Wood Carver

Green dimensions are
raindrops on leaves
for the burin
in noble woodcarving lives.

Halted flight.
Trot that breaks a meadow.
Glide of herons
over blue lagoons.

The hand dissolves the alders
of ancient forests
awaiting legends.

May the painful air move you
pincoya[32] who traverses the nights,
surely delivered with utmost gentleness.

---

[32] "Pincoya" is the name of a mermaid in Chilean mythology from Chiloé.

Barley

It is so true that the sun
has not descended in vain
for all the graces
of a sea wind that rises, flies,
becomes an accurate word
behind stolen doors and keys,
emphatic and granite-like.

We are barley, pure intoxication
of harvests, rustling of dead leaves
of this last autumn
that fades with the clamor of water,
Persian age for birds' grains,
powerful as the earth's salt,
at the warm
table of kings.

Like Golden Lemons

They are not ghosts
the galleries of your hair
like golden lemons
in the turmoil of this shore,
living corymb
of vast empires and foundations.

Loneliness Whistles in Their Keys

Barriers have been crossed,
dawn is far away
and loneliness whistles in their keys.
Like two heads resistant to walls
and at the end of waiting
raised above broad hills.

Morning Breezes

What to say, morning breezes,
you did not tell me to wait
door angles
nor balconies have stopped determined footsteps.
Not even the sea's voice was heard.
Then, perfumed landscapes remained woven
like winds from the south of Río Grande.

Whistling Birds

Whistling birds are our silent tongues
that go into exile from resentment
under calm desert times.

Last Region Among Mists

Thus my city was founded
in a vast region,
it will not be proclaimed for the last time.
The world does not stop
nor are we experts in moons.
And the navigator who sought
to reach the sea,
is at the summit.

Queen and Bare Feet

Queens and bare feet
in the terror of our world.
Loneliness and solitudes
in my language of exile.
The following dawns
will be surmountable and rescued
for the burn of your waiting
of a perfumed umbel.

The Temples Are Reached

"She wanted to stay when she saw my sadness." [33]

Wide roads of bluish whiteness,
owner of her dead,
her provinces, her herbs,
plots of potatoes, beans, and her own designs
where she returned in the great season turned into grains
with all the presumption of her power,
and praise be she
because she chose not to remain
on these traced slopes,
with us.

---

[33] Verse from the song "Ella" (She) by the Mexican singer José Alfredo Jiménez (1943).

Such Is the Instance

Such is our extreme instance.
Your task among us
was to clarify messages and responses
rainy solanaceous plant,
from train to train,
ceremoniously transformed into wheat
smiling and without officiants
for your ardent weariness
of feline times,
toward a midday without sorrows.

It has been said that there is no
higher usurpation
on the vessel of desertion.

Weighing on My Heart

The burn lies in your seas
shaped on their curves
weighing on my heart
every night
of vessels, riggings, and losses.
You are not the docile wave in its power.
Armor of luminous nets
a brew of hidden offerings and oceans.

The Vastest

Bartering
is the most expensive of our uncertain mansions,
urgent thresholds
for hasty kingdoms of tomorrow
that will never be described
even in the most closed fences,
the vastest when lightning strikes
and the epicenter marks
the dispossessed,
who will always
sing praises for your favorite violets
and your everyday quails.

Golden Enameled Body

Your body is purple wine
enameled with gold, passed through sieves,
nubile soul coated in my flame
exactly the sliding of sands.

You are the impatience of laureate stones
for the drunken goodness of tunics left
to chance, music that can be heard
on new days as accomplices.

Drunk, extremely drunk with your shelter,
I will follow your inevitable cry
delaying breezes and soft rain.

Solitude must be the heart of the dream,
of naked gold, remote, never early access
sweet foreign wisdom from the East.

Building Houses

When we were building houses
it was good to rest under the sun.
On second thought, we did not know
about building or Pythagorean matters.

The men grazed in the daylight.
Tremulous discoverers of their laziness
praising the intoxication to come,
the weekend.

Afterwards, everyone complained.
They believe sky belongs to them,
like lying down on the grass.

But that is not all.
Old explorers of streets and happy places
will return to their work as every day.

Keys

There you are, food of the night,
behind keys,
a mixture of amber, black pine groves,
and forests of green myristica trees.

A sea of harsh breezes
already drizzling and all its contours
from where it is possible to inscribe
words in all their glory, beauty, and nobility
far from rigid borders
to the engrossed seeker
of that familiar face.

Magnificent keys to a single door,
the snap of a hand seeking perennial ablutions
never a stranger in the spiniest conquest
for that time of keys
of no usurpation
and with this written honey
so that you will belong to me,
for this desire
like the earth, travels.

A Work of Tiredness: On Translating *Vast Empires*

María Paz Wallffiguer Mardones

SOMEHOW, WRITING A TRANSLATOR'S NOTE always feels like writing a letter to an angry reader—apologizing for maybe ruining the work of their favorite artist, but also trying to justify why I did it. This, honestly, might be worse. Considering that I haven't read any previous translations of Rolando Cárdenas' poems into any language, maybe I haven't ruined it for English readers just yet.

One of my teachers used to say that most of the time, translating poetry is a work of tiredness: you deliver the poem into a different language knowing it could be improved, but you feel exhausted—of language itself, of imagery, of rhythm, of interpretations; but mostly, tired of your own mind constantly debating and acknowledging your limitations. Nonetheless, while reading and working with Rolando's poems, despite the tiredness, I was deeply moved by his use of Spanish in such a simple, refined and thoughtful way, his secretive mastery of portraying those mesmerizing realms of longing, solitude, and nature as his own manner of expressing exhaustion: through memory, not as a mere revision of his life and what he saw, but as a way of immortalizing his Punta Arenas, his ancestors, and his friends. Therefore, as foreign as these translations of Rolando's poems might be to English readers, they were intended as a way of bringing the readers a little closer to a language, to a poetry that's deeply connected to the life and history of a man who was, in essence, a foreigner even in his own country, except for that little and distant piece of land that he felt like home: his beloved Punta Arenas.

Two Nouns Suffice: Truth and Beauty

Jorge Aravena Llanca

Translated by Daniela Anaís Jara Guevara and Valentina Merino Amigo. Berlin, Germany, 17 October 2024.

MY PHOTOGRAPHY COLLECTION, *Rostro Poético de Chile*, showcases the noble faces poets have always had. Through the black and white or color language of photographs, the clarity and quality of their souls are revealed. It is enough to look at Rolando Cárdenas Vera's face, the one and only, who represented the southernmost city in the world. Through his poems we get to revel in his mind, and through his portraits we get to revel in his noble and worthy face; his immortality is written into being with his hands. When I miss him, I console myself thinking that I, with my portraits, and he, with his poetry, will stay together for all eternity.

Rolando lived immersed in a duality that was both integrating and conflicting; it placed him in opposition to both nature and to culture; it put him at odds with his responsibilities to society, and also those to his own body. On one side was the world of his human needs and limitations, those laws of life by which he lived, and against which he, almost unconsciously, resisted. He was yet another man in a devouring city, a passenger in search of freedom. On the other side was his poetic universe, which emerged as he consciously and voluntarily embraced his calling—what might be called his nature. Through poetry, he became more human, imaginative, sensitive, and melodic. He sought "pure" poetry—elegant, lonely, and melancholic—as if he was always searching for the tranquility of the language of death. Thus, Rolando appears ever more clearly to us, generous and magical, as poets often are.

Rolando's poetry is characterized within his generation by his search for the exquisite and the perfect. His work strives for the highest expression in free verse, conveyed through symbols—sometimes obscure at first—but always intended to foster deep emotional resonance between poet and reader. His verses express pain, solitude, boredom, and a sincere confession of all human weaknesses, including his own. His poetry reflects a nostalgia for a lost paradise and a deep desire for a better world—one that could satisfy the soul's needs. Though these themes are universal, Rolando had the rare ability to express them with precision and authenticity.

His favorite subject was his own misunderstood personal experience, yet he held a profound regard for others. His poetry reveals a persistent, bleeding, and deeply ethical concern for human suffering. He was like an educated political figure—sensitive and inclined toward immediate action. His loyalty was unwavering, his honesty complete. That honesty became his dignity and pride.

We find in these virtues the true Rolando: a human being, a friend, a brother, and a loyal companion in solitude. But to define him, no adjectives are necessary. Two nouns suffice: "truth" and "beauty." These words capture the essence of Rolando's soul and his poetry.

In one of his last letters to me, Rolando wrote with great clarity and nostalgia about our mutual exile. There are moments when we care more for the human being than the poet—and in that letter, both are present. In 1985, he and I decided to create a book about the Generation of 1950. He took responsibility for the poetic selection and biographies, and I for the translation and design. His contributions showed a respect for poetry and poets that only men of great culture possess.

About himself, he wrote with characteristic modesty: "His poetry is rooted in his land and experiences, where the Magellanic man works in a harsh landscape, a sum of all the seasons, of faraway *estancias*, of shared life between shepherds and fishermen. Above all, he expresses gratitude toward the land and the sea." Ricardo Latcham described Rolando's work as capturing "the toponymy and idiosyncrasy of the Magellanic land and sea," where "the rain, the winter, the cold wind, the small-forested towns, evoked in the distance, give shape to very suggestive poetic sets."

His personal life was not without love. Sonia, delicate and attentive, inspired many of his early love poems. Eliana, his final partner, shared with him the intimacy of literary circles, and even their moments of jealousy became the stuff of legend. His third love was poetic and quiet—a folklorist with whom he shared elevator rides and long silences on Phillip Street.

Rolando was born in 1933 and came to Santiago at 22, leaving behind the South of all Souths—Magallanes—a place he believed was the center of the Earth. In Santiago, he lived with his "three Green Goblins" from Chilote mythology, carried in the breast pocket of his jacket. They haunted him with hangovers and melancholy but became, in time, honest and noble companions. He preserved in them the mystery of ancient religion and the tenderness of his homeland.

The bars he frequented, like Refugio López Velarde, were reflections of his loneliness. Inside them, he had no North or West or East—only a thirsty and damaged South. There, among men who shared his fate, he realized the deep solitude of having left his childhood, his home, and his past behind.

I received Rolando's final letter with great sadness. He spoke of Eliana's death and his grief: "Sing the tango you wrote for us and remember me like that, dear Jorge, like you describe me and like you knew me." I responded, but my letter was returned—"return due to demise." His death, reported in *La hoja verde*, was met with sorrow and bitterness. He died, like so many Chilean poets, in social abandonment.

Yet his voice persists. He is read in Madrid, remembered in Paris, sung in Berlin, mourned in Stockholm. His poems live on, more present than ever. Is that not true immortality?

Translation as an Act of Love: An Afterword

Martin Rock

LONGTIME READERS of The Unsung Masters Series will notice that this is a slightly different kind of book from past volumes. Rather than framing Rolando Cárdenas's poetry mostly through essays of literary criticism, this book relies often on translators' notes by those who have translated his work.

In this way, this is as much a volume of and about translation as it is a book of literary criticism. Still, it admirably does the work The Unsung Masters Series strives to do with each volume: it recognizes a magnificent and surprisingly, tragically, little-known poet. It is a book that begs us to continue asking how we might reimagine the canon, even how we might decolonize it: what are the geopolitical contexts that determine who is remembered, and why? Who gets to be included and who excluded by nature of their time, place, and identity? Who represents a language, a country, a movement? What is possible in the aftermath of authoritarian scouring?

Another departure in this book is that many of these poems—most of them, in fact—appear translated into English for the first time in this volume. The translators' notes give us insights into the music, landscape, stylistic choices, and literary allusions of Rolando Cárdenas's work, even as they offer access to the relationship and the space between languages and cultures. They open a dialogue and invite further and future literary criticism on this important and overlooked poet. And hopefully they encourage the reader to seek out other Chilean poets they may not have read.

* * *

IN ITS EMPHASIS on the act of translation and the perspectives of translators, this book also invites us to explore the relationship between translation itself and the preservation of overlooked or excluded writers. How might works in translation enable us to consider a global literature or literary culture? How can translation work against recent political and social movements intended to flatten, erase, or homogenize language? How does it enable us to connect and share across multifarious and intersecting literary cultures and identities? What can we learn from disappeared or incarcerated poets who found themselves at odds with past authoritarian regimes? What were they telling us?

In this sense, the translation of poetry across languages is more than simply communication or restoration—it is an act of love. Even more, it is an act of love for that which is different, unfamiliar, or unknown. The instinct to translate is the instinct to reach across cultures, languages, and time-periods, and to love each other across that difference. One of the many tasks of the translator, then, is not to turn something different into something familiar, but to de-familiarize and complicate the known, to broaden a reader's capacity to love what is not understood; to expand what is possible; to embrace what is different.

It could be argued that this expansion and embrace is also the work of poetry, an argument that feels relevant to what we know of Cárdenas's life and work. Perhaps this instinct toward loving the unfamiliar is why poets are so often seen as threats to fascist regimes. Perhaps this has something to do with the incarceration of Cárdenas and the near loss of his body of work. Poetry embraces difference—fascism abhors it.

* * *

BUT TRANSLATION IS ALSO an attempt at replication, and in this sense, it is impossible. Language is alive, and as a living thing, it is incapable of being replicated. Only the part of language that is material can be copied exactly. That which is alive—that which happens in relationship between a writer and a reader, or a speaker and a listener—can only be evoked, invited, experienced, or remembered. One cannot take a canary and recreate it precisely as a heron or a bluebird. But even in its impossibility, translation *is*. It exists.

And I think it exists because we strive to understand and communicate and be inspired by each other, and also because the life force in a work of art wants to go on being. The art itself is alive.

One way for the art to continue to exist is to pass part of itself along, as animals and trees do, to embed its base code into a new life or into a new form of life. In this interpretation, translators are doing work on behalf of the living art itself. The poem is something like the "zombie-ant fungus" that gets into the brains of insects and makes them climb to the tops of the trees so that they can be eaten, so that the fungus can go on replicating itself. Which would make translators, in our humility, the ants.

In this sense, translation is more an evolution and continuance of the original rather than a replica or recreation. It's less like cloning and more like mutation or iterative life making.

* * *

WHEN RICHARD ALPERT, also known as Baba Ram Das, was asked about the benefits of the psychedelic experience, he responded with a question: once a door has been opened, why would you continue to walk back and forth across the threshold? Similarly, once a piece of art has been created, what is the point of recreating that work of art exactly, over and over again?

Translation, in its love and in its imperfection, offers a kind of deep relationship to the original work of art, and invites us to understand the original as a living thing we seek to learn from and be in contact with. It suggests a sense of reciprocal community, rather than thinking of language or the poem as an object that we must grasp or manipulate until we can form it into something that feels familiar to us. Another way to put it is that no new life, to my knowledge, has ever been produced from the act of dissection.

Which is to say I've read translations that sometimes adhere absolutely—one could even say perfectly—to the original, but they have the feeling of dead bodies on the table. The poems don't feel *alive*. And I've also read translations where the translator took creative liberties, and made decisions to depart at times from the exact image or meter or line break made by the poet. And yet the poem, the arriving poem, in its departures and eccentricities, is so alive it embraces you completely, and you can only trust that it contains a piece of the living, breathing spirit of the original, or that it's in communion or communication with the spirit of the original work.

* * *

THE POEMS IN THIS BOOK, I believe, are alive with the spirit of the original work. And because the editors of this volume have arranged most of the sections so they are translated each by a different translator, they offer us a glimpse into the work of Cárdenas as experienced through the prism of other minds, even as it further refracts and is experienced again through our own. Readers of this book are given many versions of a single poet, many thresholds (in this case, they are thresholds worth revisiting) through which to enter his universe.

In this way, we're inviting Rolando Cárdenas into conversation with us, in the spirit of honoring his poetry and his life, to the greatest extent we are able. We are grateful for his presence, and for his gifts, and most of all for his poems. And, speaking on behalf of the series editors, Kevin Prufer, Wayne Miller, and myself, we are also immensely grateful to the editors and contributors of this volume for their tireless work and for their own translations of Cárdenas, which are themselves alive and which exist in living community with Cárdenas's original works.

This book, like all the books in The Unsung Masters Series, would not be possible without the support of our donors, sponsors, and partner journals. We want to express gratitude, as ever, to Inprint, Debbie Gary, and the University of Houston Department of English. Nearly 20 years ago, Kevin and Wayne had the brilliant idea to begin this series when they were both at *Pleiades*. What makes an "unsung master" hasn't changed since: "In any room of ten well-read poets, eight or nine of them ought not to have ever heard of the poets we publish. But upon reading their work, all would agree on the merit of their literary contributions and quality of writing."

Their next brilliant idea was to distribute these books not through traditional distribution channels, which typically result in maybe a few hundred readers for a critical volume, but instead to invite literary journals to distribute these books to subscribers for the cost of printing and shipping. Unsung Masters volumes are now delivered to readers of *Pleiades* and *Gulf Coast*, and this year we're excited to start a new partnership with *Ploughshares*. Past volumes have also gone out to subscribers of *Copper Nickel, Cincinnati Review, The Asian American Literary Review,* and *The Georgia Review*, when there was an existing relationship between the volume and the journal. The result has been that each "unsung master" has found a new audience of thousands of avid readers of poetry every year at very little cost other than time and labor of love.

So, like all volumes in this series, may this book be the beginning of a conversation, rather than the culmination of a life's work. As Felipe so beautifully writes it in his editor's note, may this book "open the door to a second life, perhaps more visible than the first."

CONTRIBUTORS

Mary Ann Christensen was born in Santiago, Chile but spent many of her formative years in Caulin, Chiloé, where she was granted the freedom by her parents to roam around the forests and beaches to her liking. She studied English Language and Literature at Pontificia Universidad Catolica, holds a MA in Modern and Contemporary Literature, Culture and Thought from University of Sussex and now lives in London with her partner, daughter and an indifferent tortoise named Winnie.

Felipe Acevedo Riquelme is a faculty member in the Department of Foreign Languages at the Universidad de Concepción. He majored in English at Pontificia Universidad Católica de Chile, earned a Master's degree in Comparative Literature at Universidad Adolfo Ibáñez, and a PhD in Literature at Pontificia Universidad Católica de Chile. His research focuses on the intersections between literature, culinary archives, and cultural studies, with a particular emphasis on the representation of food practices and women's knowledge in writing.

Ramón Díaz Eterovic is one of the best-known writers of crime stories in Chile, where his Detective Heredia books have been adapted into the graphic-novel series *Heredia Detective* and a TV series, *Heredia y Asociados*. The subject of the documentary "El rostro oculto en las palabras" (*The Hidden Face in Words*), Díaz Eterovic is the author of more than forty novels, including *The Fires of the Past, The Music of Solitude,* and *Dark Echoes of the Past*, the first Heredia novel to be translated into English, as well as short-story and poetry collections, and children's books. The recipient of the Gijón's Salón Iberoamericano del libro Las Dos Orillas prize, the Chilean National Cultural Board Prize, the Santiago Municipal Book Prize, the Francisco Coloane National Narrative Prize, and the Altazor Arts

Prize, his work has also been published in Chile, Portugal, Spain, Greece, Croatia, Argentina, Mexico, France, Holland, and Germany. He was the recipient of the 2025 National Prize for Literature.

Julia Guez is a writer and translator based in Houston. Four Way Books published her first and second collections of poetry, *In an Invisible Glass Case Which Is Also a Frame* (2019) and *The Certain Body* (2022). Guez co-translated *Equestrian Monuments* by the Costa Rican poet, Luis Chaves, for After Hours Editions in 2022. She is currently translating *La Mano Suicida* by María Montero. Poems, essays and translations have appeared or will soon be forthcoming from *IMAGE, Kenyon Review, BOMB, The Brooklyn Rail, POETRY, The Guardian* and *PEN Poetry Series*. For her work, Guez has been awarded a Discovery */Boston Review* Poetry Prize, Fulbright Fellowship, a translation fellowship from the National Endowment for the Arts and an Inprint—Restrepo Americas Translation Prize. Guez holds degrees from Rice and Columbia; she is the translation editor for *Gulf Coast.*

Biviana Hernández is a Spanish Language and Communication teacher, holds a Master's degree in Contemporary Latin American Literature, and a PhD in Human Sciences from Universidad Austral de Chile. She currently serves as a faculty member in the Department of Spanish at Universidad de Concepción, where she teaches and conducts research on Latin American poetic production. She is the author of the essay *Levantisca & Liberesca. Lecturas sobre poesía 1981 – 2014* (2021), the poetry collection Embargos (2023), and co-editor of the volume *La Bandera de Chile es extranjera en su propio país. Estudios sobre la poesía civil / insurrecta de Elvira Hernández* (2025).

Jorge Aravena Llanca is a Chilean photographer, writer, researcher and singer-songwriter from Pichilemu. Aravena Llanca currently resides in Berlin, Germany, and is a professor at the Free University of Berlin.

Martin Rock is a poet, translator, and editor living in San Diego. He is the author of *Infinite Scroll*, selected by Carolyn Forché for the 2025 Tupelo Berkshire Prize, *Residuum* (Cleveland State Poetry Center First Book Prize), and the chapbooks *Dear Mark* (Brooklyn Arts Press) and *Fish, You Bird* (Pilot Books, with Phillip D. Ischy). His work appears in *Best American Experimental Writing, Best New Poets, Poem-a-Day, AGNI, Copper Nickel, The Georgia Review,* and elsewhere. His translations of Japanese poetry have been featured in *Asymptote* and *Poetry International*. He is co-editor of the forthcoming anthology *Other Legacies: Great Unsung American Poets* (Wesleyan). He teaches writing and climate justice at UC San Diego and is co-director and Series Editor for The Unsung Masters Series. Find him at @infinite-scroll.bsky, @margotssandbox, and www.martinrock.us.

Jorge Teillier (1935-1996) was a Chilean poet, editor, and critic. The author of twelve books of poetry—recently anthologized in *Nostalgias de la Tierra* (Catedra, 2013)—Teillier is perhaps best known as the founder of Laric Poetry, a poetics characterized by myth, childhood, and provincial life.

María Paz Wallffiguer Mardones lives in Concepción, Chile, where she works as a literary translator of German, English, and Spanish. Most recently, she has worked on the translation processes of such authors as Christine Lavant, Lina Atfah, Ilma Rakusa, Özlem Özgül Dundar, Ann Cotten, Ina Jens, and Rolando Cárdenas.

Mathew Weitman's debut poetry collection *The Campus Novel: Poems* is forthcoming with Tupelo Press. His work can be found in *Copper Nickel, The Georgia Review, Virginia Quarterly Review*, and elsewhere. He is the winner of the Loraine Williams Poetry Prize, the AWP Kurt Brown Award, the Inprint Verlaine Prize in Poetry, and has received residencies and fellowships from MacDowell, UCROSS, and Millay Arts. Currently, he is pursuing his PhD in creative writing and literature at the University of Houston, where he is an Inprint Brown Foundation Fellow.

Poet and translator **July Westhale** was born in the American Southwest. Their books include *moon moon, Trailer Trash,* and *Via Negativa*, which Publishers Weekly called "stunning" in a starred review. Their hybrid translation project *Unmade Hearts: My Sor Juana* came out in 2024 from Small Harbor. Ocean Vuong chose Westhale as the 2018 University of Arizona Poetry Center Fellow. They have work in *McSweeney's, DIAGRAM, The National Poetry Review, Prairie Schooner, CALYX, Hayden's Ferry Review,* and *The Huffington Post,* among others. July is represented by Carolyn Forde at Transatlantic and lives in Tucson, where they are adapting their novel to film. www.julywesthale.co

Miller Williams (1930-2015) was an American poet, educator, and translator. The highly influential author of thirty-seven books of poetry and prose, including *Some Jazz a While: Collected Poems* (University of Illinois Press), Williams co-founded the American Literary Translator's Association, the University of Arkansas Press, and the *New Orleans Review.* Among his many honors, Williams received the Henry Bellman Award, a Fulbright professorship at the National University of Mexico, the Prix de Rome Prize for Literature, the National Arts Award, and the Lifetime Achievement Award in Writing, given by the Porter Prize Foundation. The Miller Williams Papers are now archived in the Harry Ransom Center at the University of Texas, Austin.

Works Cited

Cárdenas, Rolando. Handwritten Draft of "Edelweiss." Santiago, c. 1970. AE0023085. The Rolando Cárdenas Papers. Memoria Chilena, Biblioteca Nacional de Chile, Santiago. https://www.bibliotecanacionaldigital.gob.cl/bnd/623/w3-article-308797.html. Accessed 10 September 2025.

Cárdenas, Rolando. Letter to Miller Williams. 29 May 1967. Box 7, Folder 2. The Miller Williams Papers. The Harry Ransom Center, University of Texas Libraries and Special Collections, Austin, TX. Accessed 1 July 2025.

Cárdenas, Rolando. *Obra Completa*. Edited by Ramón Díaz Eterovic. Ediciones La Gota Pura, 1994.

Cárdenas, Rolando. "La Pasión del Mar." By H.G. 30 Aug. 1975, *Las Últimas Noticias.* MC0050512. The Rolando Cárdenas Papers. Memoria Chilena, Biblioteca Nacional de Chile, Santiago. https://www.memoriachilena.gob.cl/602/w3-article-84815.html. Accessed 10 September 2025.

Cárdenas, Rolando. "Tres Jóvenes Intelectuales Chilenos en el Boum de Casa de las Américas." By Raúl Mechado. *El Siglo*, 19 March 1972. RC0295447. Autores Chilenos, Memoria Chilena, Biblioteca Nacional de Chile, Santiago. https://www.bibliotecanacionaldigital.gob.cl/bnd/628/w3-article-652914.html. Accessed 10 September 2025.

Deisler, Guillermo. Engraving Plate Used for the Cover of *Personajes de mi Ciudad*. 1964. AD-00910. Guillermo Deisler Archive. Centro Nacional de Arte Contemporáneo Cerrillos, Santiago. Accessed 27 June 2025.

Lagos, Marino Muñoz. "El Poeta Rolando Cárdenas." *La Presna Austral*, 1 Nov. 1990. MC0050515. The Rolando Cárdenas Papers. Memoria Chilena, Biblioteca Nacional de Chile, Santiago. https://www.memoriachilena.gob.cl/602/w3-article-84817.html. Accessed 10 September 2025.

Llanca, Jorge Arevena. *Jorge Teillier: álbum fotográfico*. Jorge Arevena Llanca, 2020. CD0001124. General Collection, Memoria Chilena, Biblioteca Nacional de Chile, Santiago. https://www.bibliotecanacionaldigital.gob.cl/colecciones/BND/00/CD/CD0001124.pdf. Accessed, 10 September 2025.

Llanca, Jorge Arevena. Photograph of Jorge Teillier, Juan Diaz, and Rolando Cárdenas. 1964. MC0050547. The Rolando Cárdenas Papers. Memoria Chilena, Biblioteca Nacional de Chile, Santiago. https://www.memoriachilena.gob.cl/602/w3-article-84840.html. Accessed, 10 September 2025.

Rojas, Waldo. "Rolando Cárdenas: Poeta del Paisaje Austral y del Ancestro Remoto." *Trilce No. 15 – 16*, February-August, 1969. MC0013715. Revistas y Publicaciones Literarias, Memoria Chilena, Biblioteca Nacional de Chile, Santiago. https://www.memoriachilena.gob.cl/archivos2/pdfs/MC0013715.pdf. Accessed 10 September 2025.

Ruiz, Álvaro. "El Poeta Rolando Cárdenas." *Fundación Pablo Neruda.* December 17, 2020. https://cultura.fundacionneruda.org/2020/12/el-poeta-rolando-Cárdenas/. Accessed 10 September 2025.

Teillier, Jorge. *Jorge Teillier: Nostalgia de la Tierra*, edited by Juan Carlos Villavicencio. Madrid, Cátedra Letras Hispanicas, 2013.

Teillier, Jorge. "Los Poetas de los Lares." *Boletín de la Universidad de Chile*, No. 56, May 1965.

Williams, Miller, editor and translator. *Chile: An Anthology of New Writing*. Kent State University Press, 1968.

Williams, Miller, translator. "A River Makes its Way Through the City." *Prairie Schooner*, Vol. 39, No. 2, 1965.

Acknowledgements

Versions of the following poems appeared in the November 2025 online issue of *Poetry International*: "The Organ Grinder", "Interior," "Epilogue," "We Listen to it Rain," "The Visit," "Birds," "Message for Magallanes," "The Silences," "The Face on the Bow," "Herons," and "Snowing." Additionally, "The Birdkeeper," "The Chicken Thief," and "The Flag Seller" were featured in the Spring 2026 issue of *Copper Nickel*. The translators and editors would like to thank Blas Falconer and Wayne Miller for their enthusiasm and support.

Unless otherwise noted, all images in this volume are courtesy of Jorge Aravena Llanca.

THIS EDITION OF THE UNSUNG MASTERS SERIES
IS PRODUCED AS A COLLABORATION AMONG:

Gulf Coast: A Journal of Literature and Fine Arts,
Copper Nickel,
Pleiades: Literature in Context,
and
Ploughshares

GENEROUS SUPPORT AND FUNDING PROVIDED BY:

University of Houston Department of English
Debbie Gary
Inprint

This book is set in Cormorant with Poppins
essay titles and Lato page numbers.